SERVANT LEADERS

SERVANT LEADERS

The Greatest Among us from Research to Practice.
This is Why?

DR. ENOCH OPOKU ANTWI

AuthorReputationPress®
Creativity & Branding

Author Reputation Press LLC
45 Dan Road Suite 36
Canton MA 02021
www.authorreputationpress.com
Hotline: 1(888) 821-0229
Fax: 1(508) 545-7580

Ordering Information:
Quantity Sales. Special discounts are available on quantity purchases by corporations, associations, and others. For details, contact the publisher at the address above.

Printed in the United States of America.

ISBN-13   Softcover   978-1-64961-855-9
               eBook   978-1-64961-856-6

Library of Congress Control Number: 2021918703

Dedication

This book is dedicated to The Creator – the giver of knowledge and wisdom; family, friends, work colleagues–past and present, my students – past and present, and all servant leaders. Also dedicated to anyone who will read the book and aspire to be a servant leader. I need you to be a proud servant leader and advocate the theory and practice with passion and pride. This is why? Not only do we know how to serve in leading, but also show up, are present and engaged. We pay attention, never give up and believe in hope for self and the people we lead. After reading this book, don't rest until you serve first, then lead second, to change the home, community, organization, or country you love.

Contents

Foreword

I am gratified with *Servant Leaders: The Greatest Among us from Research to Practice. This is Why?* Without question, this is a unique leadership book of today and the future. As the stakes have risen, leaders of all kinds must recognize the need to reorient themselves to meet present needs of homes, communities, organizations, and countries. A simple lesson worth reiterating is that excellence attracts excellence. This servant leadership book is excellent for theoretical and practical learning, training, and character development. It entails plethora of wisdom and new constructs of how each leadership theory informs the practice and how the practice informs the theory.

Leaders that refuse to serve first are bound to follow a rigid "business-as-usual" approach, and likely to produce poor results. In today's turbulent times, careful attention to reinventing leadership along the thoughts, context and lines suggested in the pages that follow, is more important than ever before in changing our world.

Enoch's ideation, life, poise, writing and communication skills as well as his personal character epitomize servant leadership. He allowed these to unfold him, and the results clearly show in this book. The book is easy to read, just as it is easy to be with the author and that brings a sense of deeper meaning to what leadership is all about. A job well done!

Augustus K. Eduafo. MD, MS, FACP, FASN
Associate Clinical Professor of Medicine.
Wright State Boonshoft School of Medicine, Dayton, Ohio, USA.

Preface
Why Do We Need Servant Leaders?

Servant leadership is NOT an attitude. It is a context-specific researched theory rooted in positivism. It is a theory with at least, twelve (12) major competencies and deeper in conceptualization than most leadership theories such as Contingency Theory, Path-Goal Theory, Leader-Member Exchange Theory, Transformational Leadership Theory, Authentic Leadership Theory, Team Leadership Theory, Psychodynamic Theory, Culture & Leadership Theory, Leadership Ethics Theory, Charismatic Leadership Theory or Women and Leadership Theory.

Even Evolutionary Theory of leadership from Life Science studies as well as the traditional autocratic, democratic, and lesser-faire theories are sub-sets of Servant Leadership.

This makes servant leadership the future of leadership. In servant leadership, I am talking about exceptional leaders who model the way. Those leaders that touches the soul of individuals and remain on their lips in every conversation at work and home. Do you want to be that kind of leader? Then, serve first before you can qualify to lead. That is the spirit and letter of servant leadership…to serve first and lead second.

I have seen and heard many individuals talk about the difficulty of understanding research language and use them in experiential leadership learning. This is the gap the book fills. The intent is to bridge the gap between theory and practice in servant leadership studies and to bring the relationship alive. That is the only way we can find meaning in leadership studies. The past several years has brought many significant changes and challenges at work and at home. COVID has added a different behavioral, health, safety, and survival challenge. That means leaders must help individuals to manage these difficult changes. In a hosted zoom meeting with over 70 participants on Change Management, we discussed helpful tools and strategies to manage these challenges and address the feelings that emerge with these changes. Participants stated these words and phrase: "juggling of work/home," "home challenges," "pandemic – mental health," "more flexibility needed from work," "no consistency," "fight or flight," "volatile relationship," "less social interaction," "stress to do more," "serving as a model," authenticity," "diversity," "distance," "acceptance of change," and "my to-do-list gets longer at the end of the day than when I started."

With the challenges above, participants were asked to express their "Must Statement," indicating their expectations. They were also asked to set goals for change whilst learning more about themselves in the process. Besides, participants were asked of some of the emotions that came up to them during the process of listing their challenges. A prominent quote of Vivian Greene came up: "Life isn't about waiting for the storm to pass. It is about learning to dance in the rain." Most participants believed that this quote resonates with servant leaders, who help their employees to pass through the rain as empathetic thinkers. They argued that the love of servant leaders in listening to employees help them find meaning in daily challenges. These leaders make employees stronger than their excuses. And, for this to happen, the GPS route to our right destination is fairness, justice, equity, kindness, respect, empathy, compassion, inclusion, collaboration, and support. Unfortunately, few participants knew that each word mentioned was a characteristic of servant leader.

To conclude, participants shared ways they handle change on daily basis and the kind of leader they anticipate working with while dealing with daily struggles of change. Most indicated a need to work with Servant Leaders because they listen, have empathy, heal, are constantly aware, positively persuade, conceptualize, have foresight, are stewards, commit to the people's growth and builds community. Spears (2002) found same constructs in expanding Robert Greenleaf studies on servant leadership. How individuals feel at work is important for efficiency. Servant leaders make employees feel good about themselves with sense of importance at work. While some of the participants named their negative feelings and the sense of powerlessness to control such feelings; others made time forget-away moments to take the emotions out, play video games, adopt or buy a dog, pair hobby with difficult task, play jazz music, evening block of time with family, and read books that find meaning to work and life. In each situation, leadership at home and work modeled the way for them. This book provides a guide for the needed type of leadership in contemporary society: Servant Leadership! Leaders who serve first, and with conscious effort, become indispensable leaders in changing their world.

Servant leadership is a theory that places service to others as the guiding principle to grow organizations, institutions, and individuals. Page & Wong (2002) conceptualize it better: A servant leaders unlock the keys to harnessing the human potential for making the world a better place through their caring hearts and their desire to serve for the well-being of others. The characteristics of listening, empathy, awareness, commitment to growth, and building community are regularly discussed as leading to a culture rooted in servant leadership.

Introduction
How Can A Servant Lead?

"The Best Servant Does His Work Unseen" – Oliver Wendell Holmes Sr. The Poet at the
Breakfast Table, 5, 1872.

Servant leadership sounds peculiar. How can a servant lead? Follow me to old traditions and you will understand the etymology of this leadership concept. In antient chieftaincy traditions, an individual migrates from one tribe to another and beg the royals of the new village to give him a place to stay and eventually, a land to farm. Proceeds from the farming is shared according to the dictates of the royals of the adopted village. The immigrant farms, serve and build his own family of servants. Children and wives served as additional hands in farming.

As he approaches old age, he requests that his children (and probably grandchildren) be taken by the adopted village royal family and accepted as part of them. The reason is not far-fetched: with time, people lose the desire to go back to their village of origin because they have established a family at the newly adopted village and probably lost contact and identity of their old place. Because the servant has lived and served the royal family for a long time, he has inherently become part of them. Who does not enjoy others serving them with no strings attached? And, as they continue to serve, it is easy for the royals to accept them. In the acceptance process, few traditional demands are made, sometimes drinks and a token of gifts paid as a symbol of bonding of different families.

Now, in the process of serving, the servants learn to know most, if not all, history, traditions and the dos and don'ts of the tribe, even more than the actual royals. Thus, they can easily recall and tell history of the tribe when the need arises. This gives the servants oral traditional power and a source of informational retrieval reference. The oral power gives them influence in performing certain rites during ceremonial events and the influence elevates them to some situational leadership positions. In context, their traditional knowledge, and conscious efforts to serve eventually leads them to leadership positions; some ultimately becoming sub-chiefs themselves.

Thus, the old slave has become the new sub-chief by serving first! How did the tables turn? Some individuals born royals could not be bothered by many things, including their own history, lands, artifacts, information and secrets of the tribe. After all, they were born royals and do not need any effort to prove it. How do I know this? Because I was born a royal and those who came to serve and join our clan knows more of our history and traditions than myself and can easily be installed as sub-chiefs because as the elders in the royal family "goes home to rest," a figurative expression of death, the younger royals who did not pay attention might not be able to distinguish between royals and slaves and erroneously presume that they all belong to the same tribe and clan and each one can "fight" for a vacant royal stool if the sitting chief passes away.

Fighting for a vacant stool entail lobbying the queen, who can nominate anyone from the royal line to be endorsed by the elders and installed as the next chief. The queen or oldest lady of the tribe is consulted and she (queen) in collaboration with other elders nominate, orient, and install the new chief. A cluster of chieftaincy forms paramountcy and paramount's form kingdoms.

Don't forget the conscious servant paid attention to every detail along the way and served as the tribe's point of reference in information retrieval. He is now able to eloquently tell the tribe's history and secrets including lineages of transfer of power, the one with traditional contextual knowledge and could be a strong candidate to chieftaincy. Once a sub-chief or chieftaincy status is achieved, all his descendants become automatic royals. This is how servants have been able to turn the tables around to lead in old traditions.

Faith books are also huge on servants and their importance in leadership. In the Gospel, the greatest among us is the servant (Mark 9: 35; Mark 10: 43; Luke 9: 48; Luke 22: 26; Matt. 20: 27). Remember your faith is NOT private but must be public because it is part of who you are. Tom Thibodeau, a senior colleague (Distinguished Professor of Servant Leadership…office next to mine) theorized that **"Servant Leadership is good work, hard work, noble work, our work."** Simply, servant leaders do a good, hard, noble and the people's work. The last piece of Tom's ideation is important, "the people's work." Who will do the people's work? Servant leaders always answer gladly to this call and avail themselves to serve. They could be paid or unpaid. They still enjoy the calling of serving, not for self, but for the people with no covet motivation for favors, rewards, empty glory, money, or fame.

Robert Greenleaf (1971), the modern-day father of servant leadership defines it as the ability and willingness to serve first, and with conscious effort, leads the group. This is a tough and the narrowest path to lead. Why start from the bottom with a consciousness that one day, others will recognize your service as a "resume" or "Curriculum Vitae" to lead them? That is why a lot has been written about servant leadership theoretically, but difficult to practice. Do you desire to pick that piece of paper on the floor first? The old, chewed gum stacked on the floor?

Pick the shovel first to shovel the snow or the lawn mower to lawn the grown grass first? Do you want to wash other feet? Accept criticism? Do the dirty jobs? Be sent by others instead of you sending them? And why did a Medical Doctor friend of mine ask, "Enoch, are you the servant leaders' employees walk over easily"? Jim, no one walks over servant leaders (I know you asked the question sarcastically). If you cannot pick the piece of paper on the floor, how can we entrust you with a million-dollar portfolio to manage as a leader?

Servant Leaders humility and instinctively serviceable nature makes them resourceful, go-to people, friends, advisors, and the memory of organizations. Through service, they create (the art piece of leadership) and demonstrate (the science part of leadership) how leadership works by telling the old stories of organizations and practically demonstrating through exemplary leadership what has made them successful. To fully comprehend the need for servant leaders in modern-day organizations, it is prudent to look at this leadership concept from two angels: Theory and Practice. These two words are interdependent. They inform the other. The theory must inform the practice and the practice must also inform the theory as well.

CHAPTER 1
Understanding Theory in Servant Leadership Studies.

"A theory is more impressive the greater the simplicity of its premise is the more different
kinds of things it relates,
and the more extended its area of applicability."
–Albert Einstein (1879-1955).
"Notes for the Autobiography," Saturday Review, 26 November 1949.

Theory in Perspective.

In his book, *Economic Way of Thinking*, Paul Heyne (2000) argued that "we cannot discover, prove, or even suspect any kind of causal relationship without having a theory in mind." (p. 11). In a related study on accelerated learning, Dave Meier (2000) argued that lack of proven instructional theories in course designs has led to lower measurable learning, lack of creativity, and low productivity in organizations. Most things we observe in daily activities are soaked in theory. Therefore, theory either through observation, discovery or learning is important in practical learning. According to Hayne (2000), we observe only a fraction of what we know, and the rest is filled from the theories we hold. What is important is to have well-tested theory with widely held views; peer-reviewed, carefully reasoned and highly recognized in leadership studies.

Of course, common sense and daily leadership experiences are important in leadership deliveries. However, it is paramount for the theory to inform the practice and the practice also to inform the theory.

Theory Defined.

Theory is a set of interconnected ideas weaved together in a step-by-step way to generalize a phenomenon (Bryman, 2008). A phenomenon is a situation or problem we question or wonder why it exist and try to find solutions to it. Since most theories come from research, it is important to know the process of research. Research is basically an organized activity or process. The activity or process has its unique characteristics:

    a. It must be empirical

    b. Systematic

    c. Valid

    d. Reliable, and

    e. Can take different forms or shape.

The common term for the process above is called **Scientific Inquiry**, which means that we are searching for knowledge through organized methods of collecting data on a phenomenon/issue/situation/problem, analyzing the data, and interpreting the data in a defined step. There is no fast rule on the number of steps to follow, but generally, most researchers agree on the following steps:

a. Identify a problem.
b. Review information on the problem (this is technically called Literature Review).
c. Collect data on the problem.
d. Analyze the collected data.
e. Draw conclusion from the analyzed data.
f. Make recommendations for future research based on your findings.

The steps above make search systematic, which means it must follow same or similar order.

If research is a scientific inquiry, then we want the results to be **valid** as stated already. What then in validity? It means the research is based on facts or evidence. In other words, the facts or evidence in the research must be justified. You will think validity is fully explained. No! There are actually two types of validity in any research: **Internal Validity** and **External Validity**.

In internal validity, the facts or evidence must support the claim of the researcher about what caused the problem and its effect in context to the study. However, in external validity, we just look at the way the research results can be generalized. That simply means internal validity is a prerequisite for external validity (you cannot talk about external validity unless you are done with internal validity). It is when results of research is interpreted with the facts and evidence (internal validity) that we can confidently generalize the results (external validity).

Validity is also not enough in a theoretical process. The research must be reliable as well. **Reliability** means the study is consistent in method, condition and results so that it can be replicated. Here too, we have two types of reliability: Internal Reliability and External Reliability. **Internal reliability** means data collected, analyzed, and interpreted are consistent, given the same situation. **External reliability** on the other hand, means other researchers can replicate the studies in the same or similar settings. Remember a study cannot be valid without being reliable, and not being reliable means, no one can interpret the results with confidence or try to generalize them to other individuals, population, groups, or conditions.

Relationship Between Theory and Research.

Theory provides a framework, model, or blueprint within which a research process can be understood. Theory simply provides foundation for interpreting data. Different researchers have different philosophies. As an example, **Empiricists** philosophical approach to theory is that we only gain knowledge through sensing experiences. They believe in rigorous scientific testing of theories through sensing. On the other hand, **positivists** believe in accumulation of facts as evidence.

We also need to distinguish between **Deductive and Inductive Theory**. In **deductivism, theory comes first before Data**. Here, explicit hypothesis needs to be confirmed or rejected. Quantitative research (using statistics) uses this approach. Note that a researcher can never prove a hypothesis. That is why key phrases such as "It would appear that" or "it seems that" Not "I know that" or "I say that" are used as research languages. The process of deduction in research is:

a. Theory.
b. Hypothesis.
c. Data Collection.

    d. Findings from the data.

    e. Hypothesis Confirmed or Rejected.

    f. Revision of theory.

On the other hand, in **Inductivism, data comes before theory.** Here, generalizations are made from observations. Qualitative research (using words) uses this approach. The approach in inductive research is simple:

(a) Observations

(b) Findings

(c) Theory

For the purposes of emphasis, let me break it down for you below:

    (A) **Deductive Approach**: Theory → Observations → Findings

    (B) **Inductive Approach**: Observations → Findings → Theory

Thus, while deductivism is theory-testing, inductivism is theory building.

It is important at this point to introduce you to the concepts of **Quantitative and Qualitative research.** There is a clear distinction in ways data can be presented to different audiences.

It can be presented **Qualitatively** or **Quantitatively.** Researchers use different approaches for understanding the world, that is, the problem being researched. The difference is posited in the table below:

Table 1.0
Differences Between Quantitative and Qualitative Research.

Quantitative Research	Qualitative Research
Uses Statistics such as SPSS and Excel	Uses narratives (words) such as NVIVO or Microsoft Word.
Theory testing. The researcher's role is detached from the situation under study.	Context-specific. The researcher's role is included in the situation under study.
Deductive in its process and reasons from general principles to specific situation. Tends to be more theory-based.	Describes the situation and inductive. Begins with specific situation and generalize the conclusion.
Rooted in positivism, philosophy of extremely positive evaluation scientific method of inquiry.	Do not emphasize on theory at the beginning of a research. A theory may develop as the research is conducted. If a theory is developed in the process, it might be changed, dropped, or refined in the process. If a theory emerges from the data, we have a **Grounded Theory**, that is, theory developed from the data. If no theory emerges, the research would be *atheoretical*, but keep its descriptive value.
Theory-based.	Atheoretical or grounded theory.
Emphasis on facts, relationships and causes. However, separate facts and values.	Physical and social environment plays a role in the research finding

Place value on outcomes and products. Look for more context-free generalization. Focus on individual variables and factors, not holistic interpretation	Emphasizes holistic interpretation of facts and values mixed together.
Detached role of researcher.	Observer-participant
Strictly follows standardized research design and procedures.	More flexible in design and procedures.

Based on the study of Alan Bryman (2008) book Social Research Methods (3ʳᵈ ed.). Oxford University Press.

The question is, does the difference matter? Yes, it does. There is difference in epistemologies (knowing through methods, validity, reliability, and scope). Remember that is the main intent of research, to add to knowledge. A researcher is not supposed to approve or disapprove other researchers work on the field of study, but to simply add to knowledge. That said, the purpose of qualitative research is different from quantitative research. Whereas qualitative research makes their audience understand social phenomenon in a broad sense (such as COVID-19 infection rates, deaths, recoveries, contacts, tracing and treating), quantitative research is conducted to determine causes, effects, and relationships (as an example, what caused COVID-19; its effects on the world economy and the relationship between COVID-19 and playing football in an empty stadia). It is worthy to note that there is also a **Mixed-Method study**, which combine aspects of qualitative and quantitative research characteristics.

Rules of Theory Development.

Any scholarly work on theory should begin with defining the terms; knowing the body of literature on those defined terms, identifying variables that relates to the terms and forming researchable questions from the variables. In a scientific study of foreign policy, Roseneau (1980) posited that in thinking about theory, there are preconditions:

(a) Think creatively. That means you should reason beyond definitions.
(b) Distinguish between what is empirical (what is) and value theory (what ought to be).
(c) Assume that nothing happens by chance. There must be a discoverable pattern, trend, cause (remote or immediate), source, and so forth.
(d) Ask about actions or instances that brought the trend, cause, or pattern because no phenomenon exist in a vacuum.
(e) You must be ready to sacrifice initial detailed descriptions for broad observations. Don't be comfortable in the details at the early stage. Pretend to be naïve and continue asking questions on broad observations. The details will come later.
(f) Be accommodating to ambiguous situations and look for underlying assumptions.
(g) In servant leadership, be playful with different phenomenon and try different observations and possible positionalities in your head.
(h) Be genuinely puzzled. Curiosity provides passion but avoid bias in the pursuit of curiosity.
(i) Be ready to be proven wrong. Be objective; humbly admit mistakes; recognize the iterative process of research and keep your opinion to self.
(j) In research, you are NOT to prove anyone right or wrong. Your study adds to knowledge on the phenomenon under investigation.

Research can take many forms. A researcher can do an **Experimental Research.** As the name implies, the researcher intentionally manipulates or varies one variable (the experimental variable) to determine the effect of that variation. There is also **Survey Research**, which involves varieties of studies. The pattern of survey research is to investigate an incidence from a sampled population, distribution of questionnaire, and finding relations of the variables in the study. Note that relationship is different from correlation. The fact that A+B=C does not mean C+B=A. In surveys, researchers do not manipulate experimental variables. Variables are studied as they exist in their natural situation.

Another form of research is **Historical Research**. Here, past events, revolution, problem, or phenomenon is studied; past data collected and analyzed are used to predict future events. The last form of research we will discuss in this book is Ethnographic Research. In this study commonly done by anthropologist, the researcher immersed self in a different culture, observe them, learn the language, eat their food, learn their songs, and dance their dance and provide scientific description of that specific culture in a context. Ethnographic research relies on quality observation, detailed description, qualitative (not quantitative) judgment, and unbiased interpretation of the cultural phenomenon being studied.

What Role Does Theory Play in Knowledge?

We have already defined theory as a set of interconnected ideas weaved together in a systematic way to generalize a phenomenon. Theory tries to find relationship between variables in terms of cause and effect and explain the "why" to predict the phenomena. Once the "why" is established as an evidential fact, the findings can be generalized. Technically, theories are obtained from literature (what others have written on the subject under investigation) and other conceptual writings in a specific academic, social, politico-economic, or religious situation. As an example, theories of learning a behavior are associated with psychology (will not talk about different types of psychology). If a theory does not exist or a poorly developed one exist, a researcher can build on it; retest the hypothesis and conceptualize the variables based on inductive or deductive logical analysis of past research and apply it to the current situation being investigated. The technical term for this process is "from the top-down theory development" as the theory emerges. On the other hand, grounded theory (remember it from qualitative research Table 1.0?) is technically called "from the bottom-up theory development."

Theories are more applied in quantitative research than with qualitative research. Theories works hand-in-hand with **Hypothesis**. Hypothesis either confirm or refute the theory, which provide needed information to revise or extend the theory if necessary (Wiersma, 2000). Thus, theory provide a blueprint to serve as a point of departure in pursuing a research problem. This is how crucial theory is, a glue that guides various phases of a research. In the process, theory identify gaps, inconsistencies, subtle-biases, and weak points in research and recommend further studies on the phenomenon being investigated. To break it down, theory is like salt, which attaches meaning to a soup. Theories attach meaning to facts and place them in contextual perspective. In this same process of attaching meaning, theory also carries additional load of defining the research problem and identifying the rights questions the researcher can ask in the context of a specific subject. This explains the topic of the book. The theory will inform the practice in the author identifying the right questions in the context of servant leadership. Kerlinger (1986) posited that theory serves two purposes: explaining and predicting. He argued that (a) theory explains observed phenomena, and (b) can predict yet to be observed or undiscovered factors by indicating their presence.

The torchlight that leads the researcher in predicting is the "consistent" attribute of a research, which guides the independent researcher of what specifically to look for. Theory can also be pre-tested or post-tested to determine if it can stand the test of time. Pre and post tests are used for present practical application and future research, another way the theory informs the practice. It all comes together in a simple knowledge that a good theory can be generalized, and the generalization tested. In testing theories, it is important to observe the consistency between what was observed and existing knowledge, detailed explanation of the problem being studied and stated in its simplest form "law of parsimony." *The Law of Parsimony* forces theory to be stated in its simplest form (break it down) in explaining the phenomena under investigation.

Theory in Servant Leadership

Servant Leadership theory starts with a problem. As an example, in the *Leadership Challenge* book, authors James M. Kouzes and Barry Z. Posner asked people, "What qualities do you most look for and admire in a leader, someone whose direction you will willingly follow?" The top four characteristic were Honest, Forward-looking, Competent, and Inspiring. Since theory starts with a problem, one can ask, "Why do we have dishonest leaders in organizations?" This means the researcher begun by thinking of a broad organizational problem related to leaders' honesty. This should be placed in a **Researchable Question** on that problem. Any question that can be answered with a "yes" or "no" is NOT a researchable question. Next, posit a "theory of honesty in servant leadership" that could be tested in a new context, that is, in your observable situation. What data would you need to collect for that? You don't need to have hypotheses written, but you might want to consider such statements to guide your discussion. This is only for practice in thinking through what a theory is and how a researcher might explain how honesty manifests itself in leadership situations.

A researchable question should have an Independent Variable and a Dependent Variable. A **Dependent Variable** is what you measure in the study and what is affected during the study. The dependent variable responds to the independent variable. It is called dependent because it "depends" on the independent variable. In scientific study, you cannot have a dependent variable without an independent variable. Thus, dependent variable shows how the effect of the independent variable will ultimately be measured. **Independent variable** is a factor that can be varied or manipulated in a study. (E.g., time, temperature, concentration, etc.). It is usually what will affect the dependent variable. Independent variable is the variable under study…the variable believed to make a difference. Example of a study topic, *The Influence of Servant Leadership on Political Leadership*. Political leadership is the variable under study (independent variable) whereas servant leadership influence is the dependent variable.

There are two types if Independent Variables.

(a) Quantitative variables that differ in amounts or scale and can be ordered (e.g., weight, temperature, time).
(b) Quantitative variables which differ in types and <u>cannot be ordered</u>. (E.g., gender, species, method).

By convention, when plotting data, the independent variable is plotted along the horizontal X-axis with the dependent variable on the vertical Y-axis.

Even though there are no strict rules of a format for research, most servant leadership studies outline will include the following scientific steps:

a. Identify the research problem/topic.
b. Review information that currently exists on the topic.
c. Collect data.
d. Analyze data.
e. Draw conclusions (from the collected and analyzed data).
f. Make recommendations for future research based on your findings.

Brief Details of the Research Process:

Introduction: Statement of the problem, Literature Review, Statement of Hypothesis.

The introduction is part of your study that provides readers with the background information for the research/project. Its purpose is to establish a framework for the research, so that readers can understand how it is related to another research. In the introduction, the researcher should: (a) Create reader interest in the topic, (b) Lay the broad foundation for the problem that leads to the study, (c) Place the study within the larger context of the scholarly literature, and (d) Reach out to a specific audience.

Statement of The Problem

A "problem" might be defined as the issue that that exists in the literature, theory, or practice that leads to a need for the study. State the problem in terms intelligible to someone who is generally sophisticated but relatively informed in your investigation. Effective problem statements answer the question "Why does this research need to be conducted? If the researcher is unable to answer the question clearly and succinctly, and without resorting to hyper-speaking (i.e., focusing on problems of macro or global proportions that certainly will not be informed or alleviated by the study), then the statement of the problem will come off ambiguous.

Review of Related Literature

Literature reviews provide the background and context for the research problem. It should establish the need for the research and indicate that the researcher is knowledgeable about the area. This process accomplishes several important things: It shares with the reader the results of other studies that are closely related to the study being reported. It relates a study to the larger, ongoing dialogue in the literature about a topic, filling in gaps and extending prior studies. It provides a framework for establishing the importance of the study, as well as a benchmark for comparing the results of a study with other findings. Its "frames" the problem earlier identified.

Statement of Hypothesis/Questions

Deciding whether to use questions or hypothesis depends on factors such as purpose of the study, the nature of the design and methodology, and the audience of the research.

Hypothesis

In empirical research, the hypothesis is an assertion made about some property of elements being studied. Such assumptions are made early in the research, guiding the researcher in searching for supporting data. The hypothesis is found to be true or false at the conclusion of the research study, depending on whether the proposed property characterizes the elements. **Method:** Participants and setting, Instrument, Research Design, Procedures, and Research Timeline. **Results/Findings**: How data will be analyzed. Analysis should flow from the collected data, not from the researcher's own opinion. **Discussions/Analysis**: What are the anticipated implications of your study for servant leadership? It is important to make sure that the method (methodology) serves as a glue that binds the research. Finally, the researcher should make **recommendations for future research** based on the findings.

In the context of leadership studies, theories are valuable only when they are useful in practical leadership situations.

CHAPTER 2
Statistics in Theory: Don't Be Intimidated.

"The statistical method is of use only to those who have found it out"
– Walter Lippman, A Preface to Politics, 4, 1914.

In this short chapter, I will give you Dana Keller 's concept of statistics in theory formation. I understand most individuals do not like statistics, but you should not be intimidated by it. According to Kelly (2006), the world of statistics starts with a question. She posited that different types of statistics exist because individuals can ask any type of question that pops up in their head. The good news is that any question that comes to your mind, there is a way to generate statistical answer. Statistics starts with a question, not with data.

Statistics need data. Data is a plural word. A single piece of data is called datum. **Data is the who, where, when, what, where why and how**. Put the pieces together and you have meaningful information from a pile of useless facts (Kelly, 2006). Good data comes from good questions. Data comes from relevant measures. Good measures of anything must be specific. As an example, we should be able to measure 50 pounds of a luggage per bag before any international travels. A measure of more than 50 pounds per bag attracts excess luggage fee. Thus, specific measures produce the right information for decision making. However, if the selected measure does not address a specific question it intends to address; the statistics becomes meaningless in a lost context. This means statistics are vital when a question is important to an individual, team or a group of people.

Evidently, most people have more questions than answers. Some questions are more ambiguous than others, and statistics are ways of making educated guess in ambiguities. Also, because of the huge cost in measuring anything or situation of interest, statistics simplify them for researchers. Don't forget research need samples, and samples generate statistics. Samples simply mean not everyone's opinion can be sought in a situation of interest. Therefore, we will need to pick part of the population and ask their opinion, which could be used to represent the entire population. Samples could have errors. We call it "sampled errors." In most cases, you will hear a sample error of plus or minus 3. A practical example is pools in a presidential election. Since not everyone can be called on the phone or email (or even on social media) to tell which political party they will vote for, statistics simplify their responses, with sample of error embedded for accuracy. That is, if 52 percent of respondents stated that they will vote for Political Party A and 48 percent for Political Party B, the sampled error remaining ±3 means, in the end, Party A can either get 55 percent (52 plus 3) or 49 percent (52 minus 3). On the other hand, Party B can get 51 percent (48 plus 3) or 45 percent (48 minus 3). Note that the sample error figure can be anything within ±5 statistically. However, most researchers believe ±3 is more accurate to the expected results.

Does this sound quite ambiguous to you? **The word ambiguity means no known solution fits perfectly**. Put differently, what is the best solution for electing a good leader? Who is a good leader? And so forth? Is the best leader the one who takes more risks or the one who takes less risk? What data are available? How good are they? Just imagine how to make judgments and decisions when there are more questions. So, statistics finds a solution, not from the "most correct" solution, but "the least wrong."

Servant Leaders need data to make decisions in organizations and for their country as political leaders. The question is, where do accurate data of good leadership come from? They come from what we see, hear, smell, taste, touch, and sense. Do you now realize why we ask questions on many things we see, hear, small, taste, touch, or sense? That is because we are looking for good data. Thus, anything we can perceive can equally be coded and used as data. As stated already, data is used for measurement, and through a context, data is transformed into information. Yet, information is not enough. To make information useful, data need to be placed in relevant context to meet a specific need. The relevant context is the relative meaning. As an example, an organization could be described as big or small, but big or small as compared to what? Size, number of employees, financial portfolio, location, or goodwill?

I stated earlier that anything we can perceive through sight, hearing, small, or sense can be measured. **A measurement, therefore, is a value we assign for a single characteristic**. A characteristic can be captured and interpreted to find the measurement one needs to address a question at hand, but in doing so, it is clear that perfect measurement does not exist in most situations. Remember the foundation of statistics is measurement of data. You might be familiar with different statistical measurements such as "average," what statisticians call 'central tendency.

Averages have three common choices: **mean, median and mode** (5th grade to High School stuff). There are also four levels of measurement: **nominal, ordinal, interval, and ratio**.

Nominal level measures categories. As an example, political parties, religious affiliations, zip codes, ethnicity, and gender (male vs. female) are measured in categories. Under some statistical conditions, averages are appropriate for nominal data. That is, they have two variables or coded 0 or 1. If gender is coded as 0 for male and 1 for female, we can easily make sense by saying the sampled group has 52 percent female and 48 percent male.

Ordinal measurements are popular in opinion polls. As an example, a five-level Likert scale such as "Strongly Agree, Moderately Agree, Agree, Disagree or Strongly Disagree are ordinal scales. Surveys are also exampling of ordinal scales.

Interval levels have evenly spaced steps, but no true zero. Grades in a course or a test is an example of interval data. Here, remember that zero is a measurement of convenience. That means a zero score in a test means the student did not arrive at a single correct answer for the sample of relevant test. It does not necessarily mean a complete lack of knowledge in that competency being tested on. It is difficult to find interval data. Close example could be temperature measuring scales such as Celsius or Fahrenheit.

Ratios measure true zero. It is the opposite of internal level of measurement. That is why most statisticians say ratio is the flagship of data types. Weight and height are typical examples of ratios. Using ratios, it is easy to say that half of 50 pounds is 25 pounds or twice of four feet is eight feet. Put differently, we can easily form interpretable ratios. Immunizations, medical information, college records and census can form ratio scales. In the end, each of the four levels of measurement needs to recognize and accommodate the other.

In the end, data, central tendencies, and levels of measurement must be simplified in groups or clusters to make practical meaning to meet organizational needs in leadership studies. This is the only way data can solve socio-politico-religious, cultural, economic and leadership challenges.

CHAPTER 3
Snapshot of Other Leadership Theories

The ultimate test of practical leadership is the realization of intended, real change that meets people's enduring needs.
James MacGregor Burns, Leadership, 17, 1978.

Learners learn from known to the unknown, the same way teachers teach from the known to the unknown. Therefore, before delving into servant leadership, let's briefly remind ourselves of few leadership concepts in existence. There are many leadership behaviors and their descriptions. Some leadership dimensions are "consideration," which means the leader creates an environment of emotional support, warmth, friendliness, and trust. Others have "Initiating Structure," meaning they organize and define relationships in the group by engaging in activities. Some leaders use 360-degree feedback as a systematic method of obtaining input from a representative sample of people who work for and with a given leader. Note that the list below is not conclusive.

Leadership Theories and their Focus.

Theory	Focus
Fidler's Contingency Theory	Focus on control within situations and leader-member relationships.
Path-Goal Theory	Focuses on the best outcomes of productivity and morale.
Situational Leadership ® II (SLII)	Focuses on directing task-oriented and supporting relationship behaviors.
Cognitive Resource Theory	Focuses on how intelligence and experience affect performance in high stress conditions.
Normative Decision Model	Focuses on decision-making in either time-sensitive or group-development situations.
Contingency Leadership during a Crisis	Focuses on decision-making, planning, and leading in times of emergency.
Contingency Leadership in the Executive Suite	Focuses on how top-level CEOs lead their organizations and what insight that provides.

Entrepreneurship Leadership	A task-oriented leader who finds and operates an innovative business.
Participative Leadership	Shares decision making with group members.
Autocratic Leadership	The leader retains most of the authority
Laissez-faire Leadership	A passive leader, who avoids making decisions and allows group members to self-lead.
Level 5 Leadership	Jim Colins study of leaders who have reached the highest level of a leadership hierarchy.
Consultative Leaders	Confer with group members before making-a-decision. Yet, they retain the final authority to make decisions.
Consensus Leaders	Encourage group decisions about an issue and then make a decision that reflects general agreement.
Democratic Leaders	Confer final authority on the group. Function as collectors of group opinion and take a vote before making-a-decision.
Charismatic Leaders	Inspire others to think and act differently in ways that support the organization's priorities.
Transactional Leadership	Focuses on supervision and performance and application of reward and/or punishment to motivate employees.
Transformational Leaders	Creates and promotes a vision; provides high support for employees, empower, and involve employees, innovate, and encourage creativity, leads by example, ethical and demonstrate agreeableness and extroversion.
Servant Leadership	Leaders have a natural commitment to serve.

CHAPTER 4
Servant Leadership – The Foundation.

Leadership is a relationship to which the leaders, the followers, and the requirements of the situation,
including the traditions of the group, all contribute.
– Social Science Research Council's Committee on Historiography, Report,
1954. In Arnold J. Toynbee, A study of history, 12. 126-127, 1961.

In a 1967 article titled *Men and Women, To My Daughters with Love*, Pearl Buck stated, "To serve is beautiful, but only if it is done with joy and a whole heart and a free mind. Three years after this article, Robert Greenleaf, an engineer at AT&T came out with the concept of servant leadership, which was theorized in the 1970s. Thus, it is safe to state that Greenleaf is the father of servant leadership. Larry Spears (2002) expanded and popularized Greenleaf ideas from the onset. Since then, many theoretical views and scholarly works of the concept has sprung up. Authors such as Linda Belton (2018), Peter Block (2018), Jeff Thompson (2017), James Hunter (2004) among others, have expanded on Greenleaf ideas. This book is a further expansion, blending the theory and practice from multiple perspectives.

Former At&t executive Robert Greenleaf coined the phrase "servant-leader" in his 1970 essay *The Servant as Leader* (Greenleaf, 2008). Greenleaf used this term to express the way he believed people should carry themselves; especially those who were in a leadership role. This phrase, "servant-leader," has been a pure gift from Greenleaf's heart to the right people on this planet at the right time, and he expected nothing in return. Greenleaf would later go on to write and speak how he believed several sectors of society should use servant-leadership in their organizations to achieve the best outcomes. He wrote essays valuable for people of faith, people in leadership, business, and education to guide their fields of calling. Today, across most professions, servant leadership appears to be the leadership theory close to a unique standard of practice with essential professional characteristics.

According to Greenleaf (2008), the servant-leader is a servant first. It begins with the natural feeling that one wants to serve, to serve first. Then conscious choice brings one to aspire to lead. That person is sharply different from one who is *leader* first. The difference manifests itself in the care taken by the servant-first to make sure that other people's highest priority needs are being served. **The best test**, and difficult to administer of this theory, is this: **Do those served grow as people? Do they, while being served, become healthier, wiser, freer, more autonomous, more likely themselves to become servants? And what is the effect on the least privileged in society? Will they benefit or at least not be further deprived**? (Greenleaf, 2008, p. 15).

Previously, leaders "managed" others though any of the know leadership styles, which Lewin et al. (1939) identified as: authoritarian leadership, democratic leadership, or a laissez-faire leadership approach. These leadership styles appear not to have as many transferable characteristics, comparable to the inclusive nature of servant leadership characteristics. As an example, the authoritarian leadership style is when a leader is planning and shaping the way an organization is running, traditionally through micro-management. And, who wants to be micro-managed now?

According to Sternberg (2013), the drawback to this style of leadership is that the leader might not be able to see all challenges from a single perspective. Worse still, the leader could be wrong in his or her directives or assumptions, yet his or her commands leaves no one in doubt that they are in charge and their directives must be obeyed. Imagine an autocratic leader with a wrong vision. In another study, Armstrong (2012) raised a concern on autocratic leadership, citing "shared division between the leader and followers" and the fact the decision maker is normally getting "minimal input from followers" (p. 60). Compare autocratic leadership to servant leaders who listens; have empathy, act in humility, and create a culture of trust, knowing that their opinion is one out of many in the organization.

Rustin and Armstrong (2012) defined democratic leadership as the process where the leader allow individuals or group of people to be a part of the conversation, along with letting them help shape the direction of an organization. They argued that the leader who practices democratic leadership "offers guidance to group members, but also participates in the group" (p. 60). The individuals who work in these types of conditions are usually more engaged and motivated. However, Greenleaf (1996) warned that "in voting, a minority may be pushed around" (p. 81). Thus, the idea that more people having input can be seen as valuable, it is important to consider the voices that cannot advocate for themselves.

Sternberg (2013) emphasized that the third style of traditional leadership, the laissez-faire leadership approach (letting people do the work they are hired to do), allows employees to help shape the direction of the organization. However, the leader is potentially just a guide, simply allocating resources. The question on this type of leadership style is, by taking such an approach,

would employees have more power or authority than they are prepared to assume (Sternberg, 2013, p. 27)? Greenleaf seems to have answered this question philosophically in servant leadership by arguing that the leader is not separate from those they serve. In servant leadership, the leader's responsibility is to be with the people, not above them like in the authoritarian model of leadership. Leaders should walk with the people so they are in tune with what the needs are of everyone, which should allow them to serve organizations better.

In a related study, Crippen (2010) posited that "Greenleaf was interested in developing caring, collaborative and inclusive communities. This idea appears to be the heart of everything Greenleaf spoke and advocated for. Larry Spears (2000), the CEO and President of The Spears Center for Servant Leadership went through all the works of Greenleaf and identified ten characteristics or concepts of servant-leadership: listening, empathy, healing, awareness, persuasion, conceptualization, foresight, stewardship, commitment to the growth of people, and building community. Spears theorized ten (10) characteristics popularized Greenleaf ideas, albeit, from his own perspective. Spears (2000) stressed that his 10 characteristics was not exclusive but throws more light to help readers of Greenleaf's work to better understand the spirit of what he wrote.

Listening.

Most people have heard the phrase "talk less and listen more." This idea of taking the time to hear the concerns of others before leaders respond gives individuals the opportunity to share their concerns and suggest for areas of growth. Greenleaf (2008) quotes Saint Francis prayer, when he wrote "Lord grant that I may not seek so much to be understood as to understand" (p. 19). What Greenleaf is saying is leaders must listen before responding. Most importantly, leaders connect more emotionally when they listen. In similar writing, Linda Belton's book titled, *The Intentional Servant Leader: Premise & Practice* (2018) focused on putting servant leadership into practice in organizational settings. She posited four descriptive words that highlight the practice of servant leadership. "Receptive" is her fourth descriptor, which in this context is "remaining amenable to diverse thoughts and ideas; inviting feedback and constructive conflict; accessible and approachable; open to the stirrings of higher consciousness" (p. 64).

Belton's concept of receptiveness integrates deep listening to complete the model of intentional servant leadership. In another study, Thompson (2017) devoted a chapter of *Lead True: Live Your Values, Build Your People, Inspire Your Community* to "communicating deeply" to the concept of listening in servant leadership. The former CEO of Gundersen Health System emphasized on the importance of listening. Thompson argued "we will never get that deep respect—deep to the point of reverence…without great effort to listen and act guided by deep values" (p. 107). He believed that relationship between listening and building trust in an organization is key for organizational growth and success. Thompson maintained that openness to other's ideas, including those ideas counter to one's own opinions, helps in listening. His most important argument was that "listening takes advantage of people's talents, and failure to listen is "a waste of time, energy, and enthusiasm" (p. 182).

Empathy.

One of the hardest things to do, is to put oneself in someone else's shoes. The shoes could be tight or loose. Spears (2000) wrote about how leaders should "assume the good intentions" of those they serve and accept and recognize the people around them. Greenleaf (2000) stated "the servant always accepts and empathizes, never rejects" (p. 21). Both Servant Leadership characteristics of listening and empathy go hand in hand with taking the time to understand and support others. Thumma and Beene (2015) believe it is important for leaders to listen to others needs while being mindful of not intimidating or suppressing their fears. Empathy means striving to understand others with love. Lack of empathy is where leaders try to intellectualize others' opinions or assume for them.

Healing.

Greenleaf (2000) defined healing as "to make whole" (p. 37). The healing process is a wholistic idea of body, soul, and mind. It entails letting the negative and bitterness go; sustained inner awareness, relationship with self, neighbors, community and nature and service to the larger society.

Awareness.

Self-awareness makes better leaders. Leaders should know themselves. It could surprise many leaders that they do not know much about themselves yet profess to know much about their employees or country they lead. I encourage leaders to allow about 20 individuals from their inner circle to anonymously write five weaknesses they have observed from knowing the leader.

Be ready for surprises what they know or perceive about you that you might be unaware of. Greenleaf (2000) writes "awareness has its risk, but it makes life more interesting" (p. 28). What Greenleaf was referencing was the importance of getting feedback and hearing criticism. He argued that awareness will not always be positive. It could be a disturber and an awakener. This awareness doesn't come easy for everyone. Crippen (2005) shares how it takes the servant leadership characteristics of listening to hear what others tell us about ourselves, so we reflect and grow. In addition, we must have enough awareness so that when we interact with others, we should do it empathetically. In another study, Axelrod (2012) agreed with the thought of self-awareness as a great step in having the consciousness to help others. Simply, a leader cannot be aware of others when he or she is not aware of him or herself.

Persuasion.

In authoritarian leadership, when leaders are looking to get a task accomplished, they give command, and it is the subordinates responsibility to obey that command. Thompson (2017) argued that individuals want to be reminded, not commanded. Greenleaf (2008) believed that to be a great leader, one must be able to persuade or build consensus, not just dictate what needs to be done. Leaders should persuade others with "non-judgmental arguments that a wrong should be righted by individual voluntary action" (Greenleaf, 2008, p. 31). The spirit of persuasion allows free-will, to choose, when the alternatives are laid bare.

Conceptualization.

Spears (2000) argued that leaders "must think beyond the day-to-day realities" (p.4). The idea is, despite the day-to-day operations of an organization, there needs to be a large goal they are working towards. This is where mission and vision can help organizations decide where they need to put their focus. Kyte (2016) conceptualized that organizations must find their deep story, "the narrative that reveals the heart of the organization and allows each member of it to find their place" (p.33). Having a servant lead an organization requires the organization to understand what their needs are. Spears (2000) believes conceptualization is the primary responsibility of boards and trustees.

Foresight.

Greenleaf (2002) believed, for leaders to be successful, they must "foresee the unforeseeable" (p. 35). The question here is, should we not take risk, weigh options and plan for the future because we cannot predict the future (unforeseeable) with substantial accuracy? Spears (2000) offers more clarity to foresight by stating that it is the "characteristic that enables the servant-leader to understand the lessons from the past, the realities of the present, and the likely consequence of a decision for the future" (p. 4). Perfection is not the goal. All we can do is use the information available to make the best-informed decision possible.

Kyte (2012) argued "good decision making is more important, and that requires long-term thinking, foresight, and the ability to sort through the mass of detail and pay attention to what is really significant" (p. 180). To do this, Kyte provides the "Four Way Method" tool for those who are trying to make ethical decisions for now and the future. He recommends before making a difficult decision, the leader should look at the situation from four perspectives: First- acquire all the facts–find the truth to the best of your ability. Second, determine the consequences of the potential actions. Third, look at what is fair or equitable, and finally, ask yourself, what does your character lead you to do? Even with these good ethical questions answered, decisions can still be difficult. However, we can at least, be rest assured that we didn't take a quick, narrow approach to reaching our decision. Greenleaf (2002) warns however "one rarely has 100 percent of the information needed for a good decision, no matter how much one spends or how long one waits" (p. 36). Foresight guide leaders to be optimistic, trusting what they know and making the best choice available after considering all the alternatives.

Stewardship.

Crippen (2010) found that Greenleaf believed all members of an organization play significant roles in caring for the well-being of the organization and serving the needs of others in the institutions, for the greater good of society" (p. 32). Thumma and Beene (2015) added that it is about the good of the whole, not the individual. The main premise of Servant-Leadership is the notion the individual in the leadership position of power is working for those they serve. Dan Ebener (2011) believes due to this close relationship that typically forms, servant leaders should be able to "recognize individuals' unique talents and invite them to share those talents" (p.18). Greenleaf (2002) also acknowledges these talents: "We are all limited. But each of us is also gifted and our gifts are various" (p. 244). Knowing our strengths and weaknesses allows institutions to promote cross collaboration, resulting in leaders being stewards of their resources. When thinking about stewardship, we should consider how our actions today can preserve resources for tomorrow. This will allow organizations to get more out of the finite resources they have been provided.

Commitment to the growth of people.

According to Spears (2000) "servant leaders recognize the tremendous responsibility to do everything in his or her power to nurture the personal and professional growth of employees and colleagues" (p. 4). Crippen (2005) argues that servant leaders must commit to individual growth and nurture others. Here, meaningful interactions, motivation and persuasion, mentoring, coaching and commitment to professional development helps in growing people in the organization.

Building Community.

Logan (2006) writes in *The Land Remembers* that "you don't find who you are all by yourself. We find out who we are with other people" (p. 178). This idea of community is very important in servant-leadership. Greenleaf supports this idea of building community because it provides healing abilities especially when paired with love. Bredewold et al. (2020) validated this idea and argued that "Community care allows for a higher level of autonomy and choice-making than hospital care" (p. 110). Greenleaf (2008) thought "only community can give the healing love that is essential for health" (p. 38). Obviously, all the nine characteristics discussed points to the ultimate of building a community or love, not fear, and achieving a common good for society.

Summary:

Servant leadership, popularized by Robert Greenleaf, refers to leaders who have a natural commitment to service (serving employees, customers, and the community). Such leaders have a deep desire and commitment to help others. Servant leadership results in employees becoming wiser, healthier, and more autonomous.

The following are key aspects of servant leadership:

- Places service before self-interest. A servant leader is more concerned with helping others through service than with acquiring power, prestige, financial reward, and status.
- Deep commitment to listening in order to get to know the concerns, requirements, and problems of group members. The servant leader listens carefully to understand what course of action will best help group members. Inspires trust. Being trustworthy is a
- foundational behavior of the servant leader. He or she is scrupulously honest with others, gives up control, and focuses on the well-being of others.
- Focus on what is feasible to accomplish. Even though the servant leader is idealistic, he or she recognizes that one individual cannot accomplish everything.
- Lends a hand. A servant leader looks for opportunities to pitch in and help even with uninteresting routine tasks.
- Provides emotional healing. A servant leader shows sensitivity to the personal concerns of group members.

CHAPTER 5
Servant Leadership – Other Perspectives.

"Attitude is a choice. Happiness is a choice. Optimism is a choice. Kindness is a choice.
Giving is a choice.
Respect is a choice. Whatever choice you make makes you. Choose wisely."
– Roy T. Bennett, The Light in the Heart.

Unfortunately, most leaders and students of leadership see it from philosophical perspective. They forget that leadership can be seen from religious, political, phycological, research, historical, gender, or even "the street" perspective. Leadership has evolved with technology, economic, labor, social, and cultural changes for the past decades. Leadership lapses during the last decade have been inescapable. Countries, corporations, and people have become associated with fear, greed, deceit, irresponsibility, and lack of moral conscience. There is no purpose in leadership if you are not helping someone else in service. There are tens of leadership theories and ideations, but one stands tall in making followers relax, get excited with hope, and visualize the future. Can you see your president, governor, senator, congress woman or organizational leader picking the first shovel and leading a community in a clean-up exercise? The simple mantra in this question is this: If you want to lead, pick the first shovel, not the best office pace or parking lot!

Leadership theories such as transformational, transactional, authentic, path-goal, leader-member exchange, team, psychodynamic, ethical, wisdom and gender (specificity on women leadership theory) are new in relation to servant leadership. Therefore, they need to be tested by the standards of servant leadership, the master leadership theory. Do they meet the standard? Let's find some of the answers from Sipe and Frick perspective of servant leadership.

Sipe and Frick Concepts of Servant Leadership

In their book, *Seven Pillars of Servant Leadership: Practicing the Wisdom of Leading by Serving*, Sipe & Frick (2015) posited seven pillars or characteristics, that when put into practice, charts a path to be a servant leader. Each pillar labels the essential characteristics of a servant leader and the noticeable core leadership traits. They guide leaders striving to serve those they lead. Sipe & Frick (2015) argued that the seven pillars strengthen the hands of the servant leader to be effective and efficient in an organization. The foundation of this theory are culture and strategy that allows for all stakeholders in an organization to succeed (Sipe and Frick, 2015).

Their seven pillars of servant leadership are:

1. Person of Character
2. Puts People First
3. Skilled Communicator
4. Compassionate Collaborator
5. Has Foresight
6. Systems Thinker
7. Leads with Moral Authority

Below is a brief explanation of each pillar in the theory.

Person of Character

Character makes up the first pillar of a servant leader. Who do people say you are? How do they perceive you as a person? Do you serve a higher purpose while acting with integrity and humility? Do you live by your conscience or not? The expectation of this pillar is for the servant leader to be humble (wish we teach humility as a course in college) and use their skill set for the benefit of the team. In the process, they serve a higher purpose and understand their calling to something beyond themselves. Additionally, they hear the desire of their followers; work with them and achieve a common goal in a slogan of holistic care. They simply care for others.

Puts People First. Others first, the leader is second. Do you seek to serve others first? Do you look to grow people? Do you show genuine concern for others? This pillar envisions a servant leader's heart to be made visible by getting more through giving than receiving. It expects the leader to seek to become a mentor and pass on knowledge and provide opportunities for those around them to grow. Showing genuine care for others is also embedded in this pillar. This could mean ensuring safety and security or tough love when the situation calls. According to the theory, a servant's heart is made visible when team members recognize the importance of this process despite their heavy workloads.

Skilled Communicator

Communication entails encoding (from the giver) and decoding (from the receiver). In-betweens are noises, which could be a distraction, physical noise or anything that impedes the receiver to decode the exact meaning and intent of the encoder. So, what are you trying to decode? Are there noises or nuances in your message covertly or overtly? Do you first look to understand subordinates needs before speaking or acting? Do you listen with respect and with a desire to have a deep comprehension of a situation? Do you speak skillfully and with clarity to deliver a compelling message? Empathy is a key word in being a skilled communicator. Do you bring people's hearts and minds to the conversation through empathy? Do you invite feedback from the team, and can they feel free and emboldened to be critical friends with useful feedback? And are you open to hearing constructive feedback and have the courage to act?

Compassionate Collaborator

Do you build only in-group members in your team and have some out-group members? Wrong – not compassionate! Do you invite others into creating solutions? Do you build collaborative teams and communities? Do you relate well to people from diverse backgrounds, and manages disagreements effectively? If you responded yes to all the questions, then you are a compassionate collaborator. The servant leader serves as a glue to each team member, who comes in with unique personality and demeanor. Compassionate collaborators build trust in organizations in two ways: being available, and not standing in people's way.

They work smart in creating effective groups with high standards; communicates effectively, takes part in group norms and activities, collaborate in decision-making, and solve problems creatively. The compassionate collaborator incorporates diverse backgrounds in building teams. They know and understand that having people from different backgrounds involved in brainstorming ideas is the best way to move organizations in gaining competitive edge.

Foresight

Foresight leaders see far than others. They are visionary and creative in making courageous decisions. Foresight has a blueprint of taking a look at history (the past) and the current situation (the present) and predicting future outcomes. Building on foresight, a servant leader should put together a clear vision that others are able to believe in and follow. A vision for an organization clearly outlines whom it serves and how it will serve the intended audience. A servant leader with foresight harnesses and nurtures the power of creativity in bringing the best of employees. Foresight leaders also act with decisiveness. Sipe and Frick's (2015) argued that the courageous actions put servant leaders in the spotlight for criticism, but the criticism paves the way for possible significant breakthrough.

Systems Thinker.

System thinkers know how complex systems of an organization works together in a flux; the same way they understand how complex parts of the human body works together. They are comfortable with complexity and demonstrates adaptability in considering what would be of greater good for the team and the organization. System thinkers have a way of seeing the different functions and department of an organization weaved together into an integrated whole. They are instinctively aware of the system and the connections between the moving parts and the resources needed to make the system work. They adapt to the complex system in fluid and dynamics situations, in change processes and in sense of urgencies. They are prepared to accept and appreciate change and implement change strategies by fostering a supportive climate through regular communication, listening, acknowledging the difficulty in change, and celebrating change.

Leads with Moral Authority

Morality is superior to legality. What the leader does when no one is watching constitutes morality. They do this by accepting and delegating responsibility, sharing power and control, and creating a culture of transparency, probity, and accountability. According to Sipe and Frick's (2015), it is the other six pillars that lead to the seventh. That is, Person of Character, Putting People First; being a Skilled Communicator, Compassionate Collaborator, having Foresight, and a Systems Thinker leads to moral authority. As an example, trust is an essential component of being able to accept and delegate responsibility, and trust begins with the leader's character.

The servant leader gives loving guidance to followers to accomplish tasks and trusts them fully. They take and complete tasks that are in their area of responsibility. Power does not drive servant leaders. They know power is given, not grabbed and its sustenance depends on relationship with followers. They like to share achievements; takes blame for the wrong, and even prefer that others get credit for successes. It is through these pillars and moral principles that leaders and the people are held accountable. **Organizations can have rules, policies, and procedural manuals, but it is the base of moral values that define how they function.** Without the base, there cannot be pace of having quality standards that come from the deep values. In applying the seven pillars, the authors argued that employees would benefit from the opportunity to set and judge benchmarks that indicate top performance.

Greenleaf Litmus Test of This Theory

Robert Greenleaf's (2008) positionality of testing servant leaders was based on the following questions:

(a) "Do those served grow as persons?

(b) Do they become healthier?

(c) Do they become wiser?

(d) Do they become freer?

(e) Are they more autonomous? And

(f) Are they more likely to themselves become servants?

It appears that these pillars could answer yes to most of the questions. Clearly, leaders are more likely to become servants themselves when they recognize the value and contributions of those that have helped them.

The servant leader's use of the seven pillars of servant leadership to properly plan, implement, and execute success are based on possible theoretical bases of understanding the research, bringing the team together, understanding the unique needs of the organization and team, and implementing technology to support the process and organizations. Technology can be an essential part of the overall process to ensure that targets are being properly met. Data sharing systems could enable transparency of resource utilization and deepen trust between stakeholders. Documentation in these systems will also provide evidence of the success of strategies and interventions. These pillars could be implemented in institutions, corporate organizations, nonprofit organizations or in health organizations that are attempting to implement change processes. There is now enough evidence that supports the moral imperative of onboarding processes, recruiting, and training and establishing pathways for addressing organizational needs. Leaders should ensure that they are considering characteristics that make up the seven pillars of servant leaders into their planned process. A servant's heart will guide them in partnering with team members to create an effective process for success.

Why the Servant Leader is Different.

Many times, the servant-leader has no formal recognition. The leader in many times do not crave for attention or recognition and focuses the spotlight on the team members to show success.

Benefits of Servant Leadership.

- Higher engagement, which leads to high performance of the team.
- Team members feel valued.
- They feel the leader cares about them and their well-being.
- Team demonstrates high morale through guidance by a moral compass.
- This leader leads with high integrity; focuses on the good of the organization.
- Leader focus on team members.
- Leader concerned with stakeholders and exhibits high degree of self-awareness.

Further Thoughts.

a. Self-Awareness. Leaders should "know thyself." They should know their passion, strengths, weaknesses, emotions, when to cry and when to smile. Most importantly, when to serve and when to lead. In the end, self-awareness makes leaders learn from their mistakes.

b. Stewardship. A steward holds a position in trust. The office or position does not belong to the steward, and he or she understands the accountability piece to the owners. Therefore, proper stewardship is demonstrated by taking responsibility and accountability. Stewards lead by example and are willing to do anything they ask their subordinates to do. They obey the rules and regulations and set norms with the team.

c. Listening. Leaders must speak in a way other people would love to listen to them. According to the International Listening Association, listening is the attending, receiving, interpreting, and responding to messages presented aurally/to the hearing. Listening leverages more than just one of our senses. Verbal communication relates to more than just the spoken word. According to Cogen (2017), the spoken word is only 35% of the intended meaning. The remaining 55% of communication is through body language.

On average, an individual listen to 450 words per minute, despite only speaking an average of 150 words per minute. On average, you only process about 13 to 25 percent of what you hear. Take a moment and think about that.

CHAPTER 6
Servant Leadership and Building Community

Above all we need, particularly as children, the reassuring presence of a visible community,
an intimate group that unfolds us with understanding of love,
and that becomes an object of our spontaneous loyalty,
as a criterion and point of reference for the rest of the human race
– Lewis Mumford (1895-1990). The Transformation of Man, 8.4, 1956.

In James Krile book, *The Community Leadership Handbook: Framing Ideas, Building Relationships and Mobilizing Resources* (2006), the relationship between servant leadership and community work are clearly pointed out and detailly explored. The practicality of the construct of building community, as a servant leader, is established practically in community work as well. Here, those whose lives of leadership guide this journey in practical ways in organizations and legions of volunteers who give unselfishly of their time and energy in serving is assured.

In another development, Larry Spears (2002), who worked closely with the work of Robert Greenleaf at the Robert Greenleaf Center for Servant Leadership posited ideas about the relationship between servant leadership and community building. He worked editing the writings of Greenleaf. One of the ten characteristics of the servant leader included building community. Spears believed that it was especially important that individuals be connected to their local communities (van Dierendonck, 2011). As a community, the need for connection should not diminish. It should be rekindled and given freely. A community that has connections and individuals who are engaged will build the strength that is a foundational characteristic of servant leadership.

Krile (2006) posited techniques to help a community develop compelling vision statements; set priorities and achieve challenging goals. These he labeled as tools for framing ideas, which include: (a) identifying community assets by solving the puzzle of their challenges while homing in their strengths and opportunities, (b) assessing available community data using any list of resources available to identify facts about the community, (c) doing appreciative inquiry by focusing on what is working in the community and why? This aids in planning for the future because appreciative inquiry breaks the cycle of bad happenings in the community, (d) visioning in answering key questions important to the community, and (e) translating vision into action to achieve set goals.

Krile (2006) theorized steps in listening to create shared meaning: (a) Identifying ways to create shared meaning, (b) Evaluating your communication skills, and (c) Planning to develop your communication skills (P. 88). He contended that the right way to identify and create shared meaning begins with attentiveness; concentrating on the speaker while still paying attention to every detail, demonstrating interest nonverbally, motivating the speakers by asking open-ended or clarifying questions; avoiding interactions and providing clarification through paraphrasing and summarizing. In step two, he argued that community workers must also evaluate their own communication skills to help determine how effectively they are speaking to enhance effective community listening. In the last step, community workers should plan to develop communication skills to improve the community's ability to concrete on specific issues being discussed.

Concentration in listening is also included in Kent Keith's seven key practices of servant leadership (2010).

Research in community work seeks to examine two aspects: (a) assessing how a greater sense of connection, service and feelings of community engagement grows amongst the individual group members, and (b) examining how community organizations see a more streamlined approach to delivering services without duplication of services. Servant Leadership set the foundation for these two aspects of research. The servant leader helps the community to enhance the lives of those that live there through service. Moreover, servant leaders are dedicated to engaging and inspiring others to work toward the common good and to meet the legitimate needs of others. Many community members do not understand or know the concepts of servant leadership. This is an opportunity, not a problem. An opportunity to teach community leaders, opinion leaders and members the concepts of Servant Leadership, which opens the door to increased engagement amongst those that serve in the community. This increased engagement could lead to new initiatives founded by several community leaders or donors.

Building Community – A Key Servant Leadership Competency

Communities have an important impact in the lives of those living together. Over time, relationships within communities have declined. Robert Putnam examined this issue and found that society has become less connected to each other. Social Capital has significantly diminished. Neighbors talk less and less with one another (as the author observed during the enumeration of the 2020 census). Even with proxy census, some apartments with opposite doors had people who have lived there for over three years and do not know their neighbor. That demonstrates people living isolated lives in which friendships have decreased. Even though most advanced countries such as USA and Europe are individualistic societies, the isolation gap keeps widening. Even family members are spending less and less time together. More work demands, the draw on time through technology, and the constant desire for more material things have led to this decline in social capital (Putman, 2000). Throw in COVID from 2020 and the isolation is quite scary. This could trigger many psychological challenges such as drug and alcohol abuse or even suicide.

Robert Greenleaf spoke to the impact of this decline wondering, "If community itself is lost in the process of development, will what be put in its place survive? (Greenleaf, 2002, p. 50). This question requires one to ponder on the quality of the community in which they live. Greenleaf continued, "All that is needed in rebuild community as a viable life form for large numbers of people is for enough servant-leaders to show the way, not by mass movements, but by each servant-leader demonstrating his or her own unlimited liability for a quite specific community-related group" (Greenleaf, 2002, p. 53.)

In a related study, Gardner (1996) argued this way: "We know that where community exists it conveys upon its members identity, a sense of belonging, and a measure of security. It is in communities that the attributes that distinguish humans as social creatures are nourished. Communities are the ground-level generators and preservers of values and ethical systems. The ideas of justice and compassion are nurtured in communities" (Gardner, 1996, p. 6).

Building a better community does improve the overall success of the organizations within the community. In order to build a better organization, leaders are encouraged to be active in the communities in which they reside (Schudson,1998). This active engagement helps leaders to have a better understanding of how they fit into the community (Donaldson and Dunfee,1999).

"Finally, the idea of the leader as servant is not limited to employees or internal stakeholders. With it comes a strong sense of community and thereby a much broader focus on the other stakeholders (including the environment and future generations). A servant leader pursues a vision and respective goal that are compatible with the needs and interests of all relevant stakeholders and that should be shared with followers" (Maak, 2006, p. 110).

One might ask, what exactly is the role of the servant leader and how does it relate to the community? Saundra J. Reinke proposed the following definition: "A servant-leader is one who is committed to the growth of both the individual and the organization, and who works to build community within organizations" (Reinke, 2004, p. 33). Reinke's ideas support the fact that a sense of strong community is important not only in communities, but also in the organizations and amongst individuals. Moreover, Skogan (2013) argued that the function of a leader is to develop more leaders. And the process of developing more leaders means the members within the servant-led community group will work to build more leaders in their workplaces, organizations, congregations, and circles of influence. Like a pebble in the water, the ripple effect builds stronger organizations and communities.

In the book *Living Leadership*, Hall (1991) writes that "Doing menial chores does not necessarily indicate a servant leader. Instead, a servant leader is one who invests himself or herself in enabling others, in helping them be and do their best." (P. 14). Page and Wong (2000) also write that, "In addition, servant-leadership should not be equated with self-serving motives to please people or to satisfy one's need for acceptance and approval. At the very heart of servant-leadership is the genuine desire to serve others for the common good. In servant-leadership, self-interest gives way to collective human development" (P. 2). Servant-led community group needs to work to devote themselves to the collective good of the community members who live there.

Spears (2004) also spoke of the focus on meaning and passion in servant leadership. This passion and meaning are important for community members as they work together for the common good. Serving first is the top priority for servant leaders. As community members work toward a better future and a stronger community, serving must be the main goal of those leaders. Greenleaf wrote, "The difference manifests itself in the care taken by the servant-first to make sure that other people's highest priority needs are being served. The best test, and difficult to administer, is: do those served grow as persons; do they, while being served, become healthier, wiser, freer, more autonomous, more likely themselves to become servants? And what is the effect on the least privileged in society; will they benefit, or, at least, will they not be further deprived?" (Greenleaf, 1970, p. 15). As the servant-led community groups continue the work of the common good, these questions will set the table for the measure of success of the group and an improved community.

Servant Leaders Harm No One.

It is imperative to look deeper into the concept of whether those being served grow in a safe and harmless environment. According to Matthew Kincaid, not causing harm is not enough for the servant leader. Servant leaders, "are expected to contribute positively to society." (Kincaid, 2012, p. 155). Linden (2008) also highlighted components of servant leadership. One of these included creating value for the community. This was explained as, "A conscious, genuine concern for helping the community" (Linden, 2008, p. 162). This genuine concern for helping the community is one of the driving forces of the work of a servant-led community. The leader should then focus on adding value through the work they do.

In a similar development, Celeste DeSchryver Mueller spoke of how servant leadership principles should develop a model to, "share learning with mutual growth and peer accountability that can deepen leaders' capacity and capability" (DeSchryver Mueller, 2011, p. 21). The article went on to highlight many of the concepts spoken of earlier. Strategies like listening for understanding, building consensus, and working toward the common good for all are important doctrine for implementing servant leader practices DeSchryver Mueller, 2011). As groups establishes themselves as a servant-led community, it will be important to hold onto the structure of the communities of practice. DeSchryver Mueller explains these communities of practices that Etienne Wenger outlined as "groups of people who share a concern, a set of problems, or a passion about a topic and who deepen their knowledge and expertise in this area of interacting on an ongoing basis" (Wenger, 2002, p. 4). Any community group should support that common concern in identifying gaps in the community and finding resources to meet those gaps.

Health Benefits of Servant Leadership.

Tight knit communities also have an impact on the health on the residents. Mimi Guarneri wrote of her work as a cardiologist and the patients she has treated. Those with a strong sense of community had a lesser chance of having heart complications such as a heart attack or the need for surgery. Guarneri also wrote how people need other people and are tribal in nature. These connections with other people help keep us healthier (Guarneri, 2006). Sebastian Junger also made the case for the health impacts of closely-knit communities. "Poor people are forced to share their time and resources more than wealthy people are, and as a result they live in closer communities. Financial independence can lead to isolation, and isolation can put people at a greatly increased risk of depression and suicide" (Junger, 2016, p. 21). These health facts support the impact relationships within communities have on one another.

Isolation is a trigger that can lead to loneliness which ultimately can lead to poor health. Peter Block (2008) wrote of the need to transform communities into caring for the common good rather than focusing on self-interest. This transformation can take anxiety away and be replaced with connectedness and caring. When one commits to living in community, it is a blessing. "We share this as an act of community; As a sign of the covenant, we have made with one another: To sustain, support, encourage, and love one another" (Fulghum, 1995, p. 84).

The Positive Impact of Servant Leadership

Positive change within the community is possible when guided by Servant Leaders. "The promotion and application of Servant Leadership in our lives and in the lives of others has the potential to positively change the world" (Baldner, 2012, p. 27). This impact on the greater good moves beyond just the immediate community into the greater global community as well. Starting small and touching lives enforces the ripple effect and reaches far corners of the world.

With the choice to lead using the servant leadership model, the leader is making a conscious choice to serve first, and then lead. Blanchard and Broadwell (2018) speak of a conscious capitalist organization and the concepts that drive them.

1. They operate with a purpose other than profit maximization as their reason for being.
2. They seek to create value for all stakeholders, not just shareholders.
3. Their leaders are motivated by service to the company's purpose and its people, not by power or personal enrichment.
4. They strive to build cultures infused with trust, openness, and caring instead of fear and stress." (p. 20).

With these guiding principles as a foundation, the servant-led community will change the culture of the community.

Peter Block spoke of the work of small groups in transforming the future. "Small groups have the most leverage when they meet as a part of a larger gathering" (Block, 2008, p.93). The future of the work for this group will include small groups leading the work of action steps that will be identified. Block went on to say that "The small group gains power with certain kinds of conversations. To build community, we seek conversations where people show up by invitation rather than mandate and experience an intimate and authentic relatedness" (Block, 2008 p. 93). This rather small group of committed, engaged, motivated members can create a preferred community that works toward the common good. The members themselves need to have shared growth and engagement. As the group continues to learn more Servant Leadership concepts, they will only become more successful at building community, meeting the needs of those living in their neighborhood, and then grow themselves as individual Servant Leaders.

Block summarized the overall premise of his writings with the following statements. "Build the social fabric and transform the isolation within our community into connectedness and caring for the whole" (Block, 2008 p. 177). One of the future steps a community group need to take is the assessment of the resources in the community. Block (2008) posited a shift of conversations from the problems of community to the possibility of communities (p. 177). This focus on service commits to creating a future distinct from the past" (Block, 2008, p.177). This ultimately leads to a stronger community who are connected to one another in meeting the needs of the common good. One area for further study would be the overall health and wellbeing of the community. This study did not take into consideration the overall health of the community. There is no gauge to measure this. If the group is focusing on the common good, one would expect that the overall health and wellbeing of all members of the community would improve. This would be due to the additional resources and the greater sense of belonging within the community. The commitment to the common good would also help raise the wellness of the community and better reach the underserved and those on the margins of society. Seeking to improve the lives of all is the work of the servant.

CHAPTER 7
Servant Leadership and Values

"Authentic values are those by which a life can be lived, which can form a people that
produces great deeds and thoughts."
– Allan Bloom (1930-19920).
Values -The Closing of the American Mind:
How Higher Education Has Failed Democracy and Impoverished the Souls of Today's
Students, 1987.

Values are principles, standards or quality considered worthwhile for individual, group, or community. Without values, individual deeds and thoughts suffer. The wrong deeds and thoughts continue into organizations just like being in the wrong lane of a track and field event. We know the results. Lawsuits, poor services, failure of organizations and liquidations. On the other hand, when an organization infuse the right values in the hearts of employees (from value-based educational institutions), they become prosperous and successful. Core values, by definition, are the fundamental beliefs and practices in which a company uses to carry out their everyday function (Thompson, 2017; Tocquigny and Butcher, 2012). Values are espoused in vision and mission statements of organizations. Many people confuse a company's Mission Statement and the Vision Statement, which is understandable since the two statements often go with one another. However, a Vision Statement should be a short description of where the company wishes to go, something easy for leaders to adhere to and employees to get behind. "The mission is the 'what' and the 'how', and the vision is the 'why'" (Law, 2019).

Leadership sets those fundamental beliefs in motion. Employees who want to work for such organizations must abide by those fundamental beliefs. Values control behavior because individuals act on, they believe really matters; the right and good thing to do. Servant leaders initiates and influence core values. This is because the process begins with the values of the leader, and servant leaders do not lack values. Tocquigny and Butcher (2012) chronicled how core values of Procter & Gamble transformed leadership of Fortune 500 Companies in the United States. Rick Tocquigny worked at Procter & Gamble from 1977 to 2010; immersed and surrounded by their core values centered externally and strategically on consumers' needs and wants, and on brands, products, and innovation to improve consumers' lives. Bottom line: Values guide behaviors of all stakeholders and with each other. Therefore, values are a compass to vision and mission. They direct an organization to its consistent, profitable, endurance and safest destination. For experiential learning and practicability, we provide core values of different organizations for readers to understand how these values have propelled them into one of the best organizations in the world. This chapter analyzes the core values of these organizations and points out how the values have practically made them successful:

Mayo Clinic, 3M, Applebee's, Cisco, Telsa, Ford Motors, Trane Technologies, McDonalds, Kwik Trip, Walmart, Starbucks, Coca Cola, Kohls, UPS, Chick-fil-a, Hobby Lobby and Google. We will examine the listed companies in batches.

The first three are Mayo Clinic, Minnesota Mining and Manufacturing (3M) and Applebee's. Mayo is a healthcare provider; 3M manufactures a wide range of products, including abrasives, adhesive tapes, and consumer-electronics components. Applebee's is multiple-chain restaurant in the United States. We thought these three companies were different and it would be interesting to compare their core values against each other. Mayo Clinic core values are commonly known as an acronym RICHTIES. (Mayo Clinic, 2021): Respect, Integrity, Compassion, Healing, Teamwork, Innovation, Excellence and Stewardship. Employees working for Mayo Clinic and wanting to keep their jobs are expected to demonstrate these core values. Mayo Clinic is very driven to collaborate amongst the enterprise to ensure that patients are receiving the best care. Staff works endlessly to help each other out to reach their career and life goals. One of the best things Mayo Clinic does to help build teamwork is by having a personal connection. During meetings employees are engaged in "coffee chat" time for a moment of the meeting. This helps employees feel a personal connection and is a great reminder that while everyone is striving for the organization needs, everyone is human.

For 3M, their core values are: Collaboration, Innovation, Perseverance, Passion for Change, Integrity and Honesty. Their values are great for building teamwork because, like Mayo Clinic, they are really focused on working together. (3M, 2021). Collaboration helps staff work together in daily tasks. The passion of change will cause everyone to determine issues, improvement areas and to brainstorm ways to make the vision comes true. Applebee's core values are: Integrity, Excellence, Innovation, Accountability, Inclusion, Trust and Community. Our research found that Applebee's specifically calls their consumers, the community, in their values (Applebee's, 2021). When the consumer is put on the spotlight like this, especially in a restaurant, it helps remind staff to help each other out delivering excellent customer service. They also had accountability listed. While this does seem individually based, we felt staff would help each other out so they are able to be successful in delivering quality service each day.

The next three set of organizations we picked were Cisco System, Telsa (the parent corporation), and Ford Motor Company. Cisco Systems manufactures many high-level networks routing hardware solutions, and a case could be made on how the internet is built on its devices. Many people know Tesla manufactures electric cars, but it is also the parent company to a leader in the production of solar panels, an aerospace technologies company, and at one a time, a flame thrower production company. Ford manufactures several different types of motor vehicles and the parent company to several smaller car and truck companies. We had little connection to any of these three companies, but we chose them to demonstrate how they use their unique core values.

Cisco – Cisco, in 2018 joined several other tech companies, global producers, and financial organizations that signed a joint business statement released by the Human Rights Campaign in support of transgender rights and equality. One of Cisco's core values is *to connect everything, innovate everywhere, and benefit everyone*, which is fitting for a company whose business is to create network connection devices. However, Cisco's Executive Vice President and Chief People Officer, Francine Katsoudas, believes Cisco's core values require the company to leverage its influences on society to achieve those goals for everyone. Cisco has taken stances for inclusion and safe spaces for employees opposed (by threatening to close offices over) bathroom bills in North Carolina and cover legal costs to those who support equality in Texas.

Tesla–Tesla CEO Elon Musk, in January 2021, gave Khan Academy $US5million through his dividends funded Musk Foundation. At the time, Musk stated this type of investment would allow future Elon Musks to be able to tap their potential and help everyone up-level civilization (Mercury News, 2021). While the donation created a lot of public relations hype, the reality is Musk diverted his Tesla stock payouts to follow the core values of the company he founded. One of Tesla's core values states that both personal and professional successes must happen by always learning. A $US5million donation will break neither Musk nor his foundation's budget. Still, the contribution shows that Musk, Tesla, and the foundation are attempting to follow the company's core value on the importance of education.

Ford- Ford's founder Henry Ford was a known Anti-Semitist. It is an ironic twist that in the 21st Century, one of Ford's core values is *to do the right thing.* Since losing a lawsuit and being forced to admit the company had Swiss bank accounts, Ford has strived to make amends by doing the right thing. Ford has addressed this amendment stance by working to support diversity and inclusion in its workforce, dealerships, and repair centers through its Zero Tolerance Policy. Harassment of any kind is not supported by any employee at any location bearing the Ford logo. The company has gone to court to help with this policy when unions, special interest, or dealer ownership have disagreed. In this case, Ford's actions speak louder than the words in their core value statement.

The next three batch of organizations we chose are: Trane Technologies, Kwik Trip and McDonalds. Trane Technologies is a world leader in climate control and sustainability. Trane Technologies uses their core values to build teamwork by basing their work environment and tactics on their core values. Working together, using ethical standards on all platforms, respectful communication, always looking for new ideas, and speaking up and doing what is right (Ingersoll Rand, 2009). Trane Technologies needs their company to flow from department to department to be effective. From their plants to their offices, every employee is crucial in creating a smooth flow.

Knowing firsthand as an employee of Trane Technologies, managers preach the core values on reviews and have been known to base merit increases on these reviews. Trane Technologies core values are: Integrity, Teamwork, Innovation, Courage, and Respect.

The next is Kwik Trip. Kwik Trip is a convenience store that is found throughout the Midwest in the United States. Kwik Trip is always going above and beyond their daily duties to be there for their customers. They want to be known as the best, and for that reason, they train their staff to be respectful and honest to their customers. They also train their staff to perform to the best of their ability with excellence and a great work ethic. It's rare to see a Kwik Trip employee just standing around doing nothing when you walk their store. Kwik Trip serves quality products, which are mostly made in house. Working together to reach the target goal is what makes Kwik Trip a successful business. Kwik Trip core values: Honesty, Integrity, Respect, Excellence, Humility, Innovation, and Work Ethic.

The third organization here is McDonalds. McDonalds is a fast-food restaurant with global presence. McDonalds does a great job standing by their core values: Serve, Inclusion, Integrity, Community, and Family. They put their customers first, welcoming anyone and everyone into their restaurants, and they are always helping their employees and the communities. On multiple occasions I have seen McDonalds as a sponsor for a local baseball team. They also sponsor local projects of worthy causes. McDonalds donates to the Ronald McDonald charity, along with assisting their employees with tuition cost for their hours worked. Utilizing their core values, McDonalds can work at a very efficient pace. This wouldn't be possible without teamwork. Each employee is working a different stage of the assembly line for each order that is placed.

This batch includes Walmart, Starbucks, and Coca Cola. Walmart prides themselves on serving the customer, respecting the individual, striving for excellence, and acting with integrity. Walmart encourages and empower associates to work as a team to always anticipate, listen and serve the customers' every need, and to be creative, smart, and quick about it. They expect employees to lead by example, collaborate with the team, accept feedback, and be humble about it. Further, employees are expected to accept different opinions and differences in individuals. Doing right by others and respecting your fellow associates is not a luxury but a necessity by them (Walmart, 2021).

Next is Starbucks. They're considered one of the most ethical companies out there, and for a reason. They have a mission to inspire and nurture the human spirit, one cup and one neighbor at a time. Their values include creating a warm and nurturing culture welcome to anyone and everyone, deliver the best and holding oneself accountable for the results, acting with courage, dignity, and respect, and finally challenge the status quo and always find new ways to grow the company and each other. They are committed to a culture of inclusion, diversity, and accessibility where all are welcome. They actively hire those with disabilities and provide reasonable accommodations and assistive technologies that enable these people to perform their jobs and encourage their fellow associates to be like a family, and help in any way possible (Starbucks, 2021).

The last company on this batch Coca Cola. Obviously, it is one of the biggest brands in the world. Their mission is to refresh the world and inspire moments of optimism and happiness. Their values and goals reflect that mission statement. Coca Cola's core values include: Leadership, Collaboration, Integrity, Accountability, Passion, Diversity, and Quality. Their goal is to nurture a winning network of customers and suppliers. They also encourage their stakeholders to be responsible citizens that make a difference by helping build and support sustainable communities. They act with urgency and efficiency on customer complaints, take risks, and find innovative ways to solve problems. Finally, the pride themselves of possessing a strong worldview; leveraging collective genius, and continuously learning the value of teamwork (Coca-Cola, 2020).

The last five organizations whose values we researched are: Kohls, UPS, Chick-fil-a, Hobby Lobby and Google. Kohl's core values are: Putting customers first, acting with integrity, building great teams, and Driving results (Kohl's, 2018). These values drive their purpose in building teamwork by energizing the team members through results-driven, caring, and courageous culture that supports a test and learn approach. Additionally, Kohl's is passionate about diversity and inclusion. They work to understand and embrace differences for their customers, associates, and communities (Kohl's, 2018). Their values make them commit to creating a welcoming environment. Next is UPS. UPS's core values are: Integrity, Teamwork, Service, Quality and Efficiency, Safety, Sustainability, and Innovation. All these values promote the qualities they want in the teams that they form to go out into communities and deliver products for their valued customers. They focus on a whole workforce fulfilling the wants of their impacted communities in a "right and respectful" manner. A practice of teamwork that UPS does, is consistent inclusion of ideas to innovate delivery practices. They prompt their managers to be open to the ideas and concerns of the delivery people in order to promote company transparency as well as create relationship within the workplace.

Next is Chick-fil-a. This company is faith-based, serving food chain based on the quality of service, as well as their hours. Their core values are: Customer first, Personal excellence, Continuous improvement, Working together, and Stewardship. These values play into the faith-based commitment they have in serving customers as well as allowing workers a day of rest and or worship on Sunday. Chick-fil-a believes fulfilling these values through action has enabled workers to grow themselves and work better together to fulfill the needs of their customers. The next company we researched was Hobby Lobby. This is another company that is driven by faith to serve their communities and workers. Their core values are: (a) Honoring the Lord in all we do by operating in a manner consistent with Biblical principles, (b) Offering customers exceptional selection and value, (c) Serving our employees and their families by establishing a work environment and company policies that build character, strengthen individuals and nurture families, (d) Providing a return on the family's investment, sharing the Lord's blessings with our employees, and investing in our community. In fulfilling all these values, they create a better workplace, foster a family-like relationship among their stakeholders and offer quality services to their customers.

Our final company is Google. Google is now a verb. Many of their values are still original from when the company was only a few years old, and since then, very few of those values have changed. They are as follows: (a) It's best to do one thing really, really well, (b) Fast is better than slow, (c) Democracy on the web works, (d) You don't need to be at your desk to need an answer, (e) You can make money without doing evil, (f) There's always more information out there, (g) The need for information crosses all borders, (h) You can be serious without a suit, and (I) Great just isn't good enough. Google takes their values extremely seriously and holds their employees to the highest standards. They want to work with great people, be technology innovated, actively involved, don't take success for granted, do the right thing, don't be evil, earn customer trust and user loyalty, respectful every day, and lastly create a sustainable long-term growth and profitability (Brooks, 2018). These values are key to their success.

They hire people that will fit with the culture and reinforce important behaviors. Google's culture is flexible (employees are encouraged to work when they like and how they like), fun (offices have nap pods, video games and ping pong) and founded on trust (Brooks, 2018). Collaboration and building a sense of community is one of the first steps to creating a more positive company culture. The Google campus is built to bring people together. Having cafes and spaces for people to grab lunch also drives efficiency. Employees don't need to leave; they have everything they need at the building which creates more opportunity for innovation. Conversations are usually about work, products, users, and new ideas (Brooks, 2018). Encouraging and treating employees as owners instead of machines is how they remain successful. At Google you are not only rewarded for good, but also failures. Failing is a learning tool and not a reason for fear,

ridicule, or punishment (Brooks, 2018) It is okay to make mistakes. This encourages employees to shoot for high goals and support each other. Googles trust makes them successful. The employees are given freedom and they choose accountability to get the job done.

Wong (2020) argues that a company value are the central, underlying philosophies that guide a business and its employees. These beliefs also influence the way a company interacts with partners, clients, and shareholders. In Rick Tocquigny and Andy Butcher's (2012) book, *When Core Values are Strategic: How the Basic Values of Procter & Gamble Transformed Leadership at Fortune 500 Companies*, Daniela Riccardi, currently the CEO of Diesel, a highly successful fashion company stated: "The most important core value is people. The culture of a company pivots on hiring, developing, and promoting the best talents." (Pp. 39-45). As seen from each company's values, it sets them apart and guides their path to success. You might argue with some of the core values. However, you can agree with me that without core values, there is no guide for business or employees and without a guide, we forget and loose the way.

In conclusion, any organizational vision must go hand-in-hand with the values. A vision uplifts and attracts others. To be visionary means looking beyond the immediate future and creating an image of what the organization is capable of becoming. A vision is all about inspiration, and to be inspirational, a vision must convey a reason for being beyond making money; timeless and reflect unchanging core values, and ambitious but achievable.

CHAPTER 8
Interviews: 10 Questions for 11 Leaders of 11 Different Organizations

"There is but one just uses of power, and it is to serve people."
– George H. W. Bush. Inaugural Address, 20 January 1989.

It is important to learn to be a hero of one's own life story in leadership. This chapter gives account of different leaders from different organizations interviewed on some specific leadership questionnaire and the power of stories they shared. Be reflective in reading these stories and share your thoughts after learning from their responses. Leadership is not just one subject, a single academic discipline, or a selected organizational endeavor. It is a combo with all the drama of toppings on it! Leadership is liked going on a vacation and after returning, someone asked you, "how was the vacation"? Obviously, it is not easy to summarize a one-month vacation experience to an individual in few minutes. That is what leadership is. Different definitions, models, trajectories, professions, homes, places of faith and worship, countries and so forth, yet we can poke the feelings, expectations, and experience of it from the middle. Simply, a plethora of ideation that permeates every academic field, organizational setting, and situational choices. Knowing this will help you approach leadership studies with an open mind.

To do this, I interviewed different leaders from different organizations and with their permission, shared the power of their stories. I am a firm believer in stories because one can pick just a part of an old story and the rest comes alive even after many years of the story being told. Therefore, one cannot go wrong with a first chapter of a book with stories. Each interviewee was asked the same questions. The 10 questions are below:

1. How do you define leadership from your personal experience as a leader?
2. Do you believe leaders must serve first? Why or why not?
3. What motivated you into your current leadership position?
4. Walk me through how you plan for a typical day at work.
5. How do you build relations with your employees?
6. Please explain three recurring challenges you face at your current position.
7. How do you solve those challenges? What strategies do you use?
8. Please recommend three ways a potential leader can learn the ropes of rising to the top of an organization through service.
9. What trends do you see in the future of leadership?
10. How can this trend you mentioned be embedded into contemporary organizations for success?

First Three Interviewees – All Computing Firm Leaders.

Defining leadership from your work perspective.

Interviewee One: I define leadership as the art of helping my teams avoid the same critical mistakes I have made in the past. It is crucial to allow them to grow and learn from their small mistakes without suffering from critical errors. I take pride that some of my staff have outgrown us and start their own companies using my leadership style, makes me believe I am doing it right.

Interviewee Two: I define leadership as being willing and able to support my staff while providing them the opportunity to improve our organization. I am only the leader because I am given the tasks our team needs to complete. Otherwise, there is no difference between the interns or me; we all add our names to the finished projects' bottom line.

Interviewee Three: I define leadership as knowing when our experience, knowledge, and guts tell us it is time to let someone else take the lead on a project. Being a leader is more about helping others to shine than it is about having others polish you.

On a question of what motivated them into leadership positions.

Interviewee One – I had a great leader who allowed me to outgrow my last employment, and she is my motivation. Without her insight, I would have never decided to try my hand at being "her" with a new crew of my own.

Interviewee Two– By default, I always need to serve my staff first. I am already on my way, due to the help of others, it is important I do the same for my own staff.

Interviewee Three– Our whole business is serving others; being a leader in this industry, you must serve the client, their office, the region, and the company. Always in that order!

On their typical day work responsibilities and relationships:

Interviewee One– I am always there first, and I am the last to leave, but I do not expect that from my staff. I make it a point to let them know I do that, so I have time during the day for their needs. It is hard to rebuild lost trust, so it is better to build it whenever I can by being there for them when they need me.

Interviewee Two – I do not decide how the day will go as that is what our staff do. I only ensure we will complete the goals of the day, the week, and the project's life. If I have questions or see a problem, we work it out as a team. These are professionals, they do not need me to tell them how to work, and I know that stance gives them ownership in their work.

Interviewee Three – I start my day by finding out the Who, the What, and the Where. Finding out what my three Ws are allow me to address the persons and the things that need my attention. I serve our clients and staff when I offer support rather than micromanage.

On recurring work challenges.

Interviewee One – Easy, meeting the different types of deadlines without driving my team to quit. We have client deadlines, project deadlines, and team deadlines; every day, we must adjust for our deadlines.

Interviewee Two – Preventing unneeded perfection from slowing us down. Being aware of budget constraints. Citation of sources and crediting content.

Interviewee Three – One, meeting the current need of partners and clients. Two, being mentally ready to address their needs. Three, following up to make sure I met their needs while making sure they know to ask me tomorrow too.

On problem solving challenges.

Interviewee One – My knowledge is how I solve our challenges. If one staff thinks they can do it in X all alone, I will assign another person to the task if my experience says otherwise. My strategy is to rely on the relationships I have made and to spend some of the trust points I have earned to allow me to help them complete X.

Interviewing Two – I do not solve our problems or challenges; we solve our problems and difficulties. My job is to maintain a work setting based on trust, where we can resolve and then deploy solutions to our challenges.

Interviewee Three– Patterns. I solve our challenges by looking for patterns suggesting we might have a challenge before it becomes a problem.

On how they rose to the top.

Interviewee One – Pay attention to those who inspire you. Mimic their leadership style. Try to improve their leadership style. Listen to those you lead. Master those traits, and you will be pushed up the ladder.

Interviewee Two – Never act like a dictation leader; show leadership in practice by showing how you want others to follow. Ask for feedback from those higher and lower than you. Make sure you put your time in at each level; never think of it as a step you can skip.

Interviewee Three – Learn everything you can. Master the skills you can. Know enough to know a master of a skill when you lead him or her. There is no short-cut to leadership roles; you need to learn the ropes and earn respect as you do.

On Future Trends of Leadership.

Interviewee One – Technology. I work with technologies, but I am talking about communication and collaboration technologies. COVID has changed the way we work, so leaders must master the tools to interact in new ways.

Interviewee Two– Digital technology is the future in the present. My department is slowly switching from paper-based analog solutions to purely digital solutions. I feel the next generation of leaders need to understand their work setting, but they need to envision those processes with digital upgrades; then train themselves to have those new skills.

Interviewee Three. – Understanding the new rules for listening and communicating, the world went digital a couple of decades ago, and leadership requires mastery of the latest tools. Everything else stayed the same; new leaders need to have the unique skills to meet the needs of today.

The Future of Today's World of Work.

Interviewee One– What an odd question. I think the only businesses open or not slowly closing are the ones who have embedded technology tools today. You can be the most outstanding servant leader globally, but you are worthless if you cannot run a Zoom meeting or know who can. Those who can survive are already embedding these traits; those who cannot maybe why a whole company of staff is looking for work.

Interviewee Two – Our success is measured in how long our archives can be used before they need to be updated; no-one uses micro-film anymore. I think leadership is like that; you must include the new technology and the goals of the old to survive in this world.

Interviewee Three–*Lots of laughing* I am sure the other people you spoke to spoke about something technology-driven. Tech is the buzz right now, but I feel it is too late to start now; you either did embrace tech or are unknowingly walking dead. I want to change my answer to digital people are the new trend, and you need to make them the priority; they use tech as a tool.

Summary of First Three Interviewees Findings.

- Each leader wanted to be measured by how they supported others.
- "I" was the word used the least in all my interviews. All three leaders spoke in terms that included "we", "us", and "our" when discussing success, but used "I" when discussing failures.
- They all seemed to see leadership as a role they were good at, not something they deserved.
- None of the leaders felt being passed by an underling was a bad thing, one thought it was a measure of his success.
- I had to repeatedly ask each leader to talk about themselves, rather than their teams, throughout the interviews. I feel this mean leadership to them is tied to those whom they lead.

Now, let's switch to different leaders from different professions. Same questions but different responses. In the end, your assessment will be to summarize ideas you picked from the different interviews as I did for the first three interviewees.

Health Services Leader.

Defining Leadership

I believe that leadership is the process of rolling up your sleeves and working alongside your staff to help them succeed. It is not leading from above; it is leading from beside.

What motivated you into your current leadership position?

I wanted to feel like I was making more of a difference. I enjoyed my work before, but I wanted to feel like I was helping more people and making a bigger difference within my organization.

How do you build relations with your employees?

General conversation about them, their families, and how they are doing. I prove to them that I am trustworthy and will follow through when I say I will do something. I also have an open-door policy, so staff feel they can come and talk to me if they need anything. No meeting required.

Three recurring challenges you face at your current position.

Change–It is difficult for staff to undergo change. They prefer to keep things as they are. Mainly because learning something new and challenging can be difficult.

Communication – There are so many ways to communicate that it can be difficult to understand how each person on the team prefers their communication.

How do you solve those challenges? What strategies do you use?

Change–you need to start small. Show the wins and celebrate those wins with the staff. It shows that the work they put in was worth the results. Then hopefully next time when change comes along their ability to change is easier.

Communication–you need to have defined communication plans. This would include face-to-face elevator speeches, e-mail, and web content. You also need to reassure staff that you have an open-door policy for them to come in and talk to when they need to. Or if you see that someone is not understanding, touch base with them at a later time to discuss one-on-one.

Ways a potential leader can learn the ropes of rising to the top of your organization through service.

Stretch assignments – Ask your leader for a project that is not within the scope of your position.
Education – Go back to school and get a degree in servant leadership.
Seminars – Sign up for seminars that are about servant leadership and apply the content to your daily job.

Trends you see in the future of leadership.

Working from home and leading those staff will become a much larger part of the workforce. Then finding ways to communicate, engage and develop those staff for future leadership roles.

How this trend you mentioned can be embedded into your organization for success?

By creating diversified teams to work together on projects. Then as a leader having regular touch bases with the team and individual team members to work though barriers that they may be having.

*Assessment: Reflect and summarize leadership ideas you picked from this interview. *

Quality Operations in Healthcare Leader.

Define Leadership in your own way: As a leader, you should always work to have clear goals of your own, but also a clear understanding of the people that you lead. Leadership is also defined as having the influence to bring out the best in those around you and not being afraid to challenge the status quo when it is not the favorable opinion, but the right thing to do.

What motivated you into your current leadership position?

Having a mix of both good and bad leaders throughout my career. I always knew that I wanted to lead people. I knew that I could contribute to the organization in a leadership position, but also, I enjoy mentoring others and watching them grow. For me, I need to be engaged and that requires me to be challenged. When I took on my current position, I had felt that I needed more of a challenge. This position is that for me as I never had direct reports in the past.

Walk me through how you plan for a typical day at work.

I always need to know the work ahead of me and try to look out at least a week in advance. In addition, when I schedule meetings, I try to put the agendas in the meeting invites and any relevant attachments so that I am prepared for the meetings. Then every day, I look to the next day.

I start my day by waking up and getting ready for work. Then I check my work calendar. During this time, I can also expect to receive messages about sick calls or other employee needs. I tend to arrive early at work and again check for any messages that might have come in that I hadn't seen before.

How do you build relations with your employees?

I take the time to get to know them on a personal level. For our check ins, which occur minimally monthly, there are three things at the top of their list that we review first: What are you grateful for, tell me about your best work since our last check in, and what is the most important thing you need me to know today. In addition, I have a section on the bottom of their sheet that lists out their long-term and short-term goals. This establishes a nice platform for them to open up to me about work and personal needs.

Three recurring challenges you face at your current position.

Being able to support my staff with all the changes they face every day. Staffing and making sure that we have adequate coverage for all the work we already have with relation to staff departures. New projects and staying positive.

How do you solve those challenges? What strategies do you use?

With Covid-19, I try to ensure that I always know what is going on at the organizational level and also, knowing enough about the details of the work that my staff are supporting. For staffing, I use my check-ins as opportunities to level load the work and work with my peer manager and my director to talk through the challenges and produce solutions as a team.

Staying positive, I find that having time off work to do things that I enjoy really helps. I also like to surround myself with positive people.

Recommend three ways a potential leader can learn the ropes of rising to the top of your organization through service.

Volunteering-giving back to others always makes you feel good, and it gives you opportunities for connections that you may not have thought of on your own. Accepting and looking for stretch opportunities within your current role. Maintaining a professional appearance every single day and ensuring that you recognize others for their accomplishments.

Trends you see in the future of leadership.

Being able to adapt to a virtual platform and a more remote workforce.

How can this trend you mentioned be embedded into your organization for success?

Organizations need to be willing to accept the risks that come with trying new things and acknowledging the fact that it is a PDSA in progress versus trying to make something perfect before trying it. Making things perfect before trying them causes paralysis in thinking and moving forward. Engaging the staff in producing the ideas instead of forcing them upon staff with little input is another way.

*Assessment: Reflect and summarize leadership ideas you picked from this interview. *

<u>**Vice President of a Foundation**</u>

For me, a leader is someone who inspires, guides, teaches, coaches, and supports a team. A leader never acts alone, but always as a member of his or her team. I believe leaders must serve first. Being a leader is an opportunity and an honor. You are being trusted with a team to achieve the goals of your business. This puts you in a position of needing to put your team first, and help them develop and perform, both individually and as a group, at the highest level.

What motivated you into your current leadership position?

By nature, I am an achiever, so ambition had something to do with it, as did finances, in order to support my family. However, the biggest factor for me that I believed I could make a difference in my current position to make our Foundation better and have a greater impact, both in our mission as well as our margin.

Walk me through how you plan for a typical day at work.

My day for the most part is full of meetings that are scheduled weeks, or sometimes even months ahead. The meetings often are back-to-back throughout the day, and into the evening, as I now have staff in all time zones. So typically, I will review my schedule for the week on Sunday, and prepare for Monday meetings the evening before, which is a pattern that continues throughout the week. Because I am now responsible for six different business groups, I have to intentionally check to see that my meeting schedule and activities are balanced between the businesses and their needs. Those needs might be related to financial performance, customer satisfaction, employee performance, or employee development. Once I am through with the meetings of the day, I follow-up with any notes to or requests of my staff via email, and then I get to the task of answering the day's emails. I receive up to 200 emails a day, so I have to be smart about tracking email chains and quickly getting to the essence of the question or problem.

How do you build relations with your employees?

First and foremost, I am an advocate for each of my employees. I give them credit and shine a spotlight on their successes. Next, I work alongside them - we brainstorm, negotiate, and work together to achieve our goals, then we celebrate. I meet with my team weekly, and every other week with each of my staff individually, where we talk about work and their performance, but also about their lives and their personal goals and dreams.

Three recurring challenges you face at your current position.

In the age of COVID, my number one challenge is being able to effectively communicate with my team members in a timely way. Each of us now is working remotely, and a great many of my meetings take place outside of my team. I have to carefully consider what happens over the course of the day and communicate that, many times that requires separate messaging based upon a person's role and "need to know".

Secondly, my team is entrepreneurial and considered a growth engine for the Foundation. Our work is different from the standard work of the Foundation, which requires me to ask for a change in processes or exceptions to established policies. Our organization has been in existence for 75 years. Sometimes people are not open to new ways of doing things, which can result in conflict. My team members often have to bear the brunt of that before I can intervene, which can make for some rough days for them.

Thirdly, because my team is a growth driver for the Foundation, parts of our Foundation get very excited about what we are doing and want us to run faster to bring out new products or services and scale more quickly than we have the capacity or capabilities of doing right now.

How do you solve those challenges? What strategies do you use?

My teams have begun a series of presentations for me and the other teams to present who they are, what they do, and the value to our department. Most of them have not worked together before this fall, so the presentations are not only resulting in team building, but more awareness of how they can communicate between themselves without me always having to be the connector. I think these will go a long way in helping us plan for more effective communication.

Moreover, I have organized cross-enterprise teams that include my staff as well as staff from various parts of our Foundation, to come together to brainstorm and execute on solutions to the most pressing and presenting problems, which my team has identified and prioritized.

Besides, I am intentionally carving out time to strategize and plan with other Vice-Presidents across the Foundation so that the areas with expectations of my team understand who we are, what we do, how to effectively work with us, and where our limitations lie. Similarly, I have begun to organize a small number of cross-enterprise strategic growth teams that can work together to set goals and collaboratively contribute to achieve them.

Recommend three ways a potential leader can learn the ropes of rising to the top of an organization through service.

First, get a mentor, someone you admire who is a successful service leader who can inspire and advise you. Second, seize every opportunity to develop yourself. Read about servant leadership, subscribe to list serves, listen to podcasts, attend lectures or conferences, or join associations or other organized professional development groups. Third, establish goals for yourself on how to become a better leader, and keep an accountability journal where you write down your goals and plans and regularly update what you're doing to move toward. Then, track your progress over time, and ask for help and support in achieving them, from your boss, your mentor, or your colleagues.

What trends do you see in the future of leadership?

Leaders will not or will rarely be in the same office space as their teams, and in many cases, not in the same geographic regions. That will require leaders to build new competencies in supervising and developing staff remotely. Increasingly, there will be less "top-down" hierarchical organizational structures, and more that are matrixed, with different functional groups working across departments in order to achieve goals, so that the team becomes the key to performance success and management. Also, leaders will need to be extremely tech-savvy, identifying new tools to organize and execute on their work. I am relying more and more on my new younger staff to bring these enabling technologies to the table for our teams.

How can these trends you mentioned be embedded into contemporary organizations for success?

I think that trends #1, and #3 are already becoming embedded into contemporary organizations as a result of COVID. It's changed the world workplace, and I don't see us going back to the "old normal". In terms of #2, I mentioned in my solutions how I am intentionally organizing cross-enterprise teams to solve problems or drive growth. I fully expect that a number of these teams will be part of embedding a new matrixed approach to the business of our Foundation. We're starting small, but as the teams' experience wins, it will become a more expected, standardized way of conducting our business.

*Assessment: Reflect and summarize leadership ideas you picked from this interview. *

Vice President of a Major Bank

Leadership to me is taking my experiences and knowledge and using those to guide others to do better. Being a leader is building trust by being unselfish, transparent, and a good listener. It is taking the time to understand your peer's or employee's perspective and, with their help, utilizing that to do the next right thing for that person and the company. Being a leader isn't always fun, a leader needs to make tough decisions, and be comfortable having crucial conversations when changes need to be made. Leaders must serve first. Servant leadership, I believe, is needed to build trust. When a leader is willing to put in the work to develop their team, guiding and teaching them along the way, it sets the stage for success.

What motivated you into your current leadership position?

I thoroughly enjoy working with and coaching others. I'd love my legacy to be that those I have helped turn around and use their leadership skills to help others.

Walk me through how you plan for a typical day at work.

Working at a financial institution, has is no "typical" day. We learn to work around the needs of our customers and staff. I organize items by importance, and I will have a list of three things that need to be accomplished by the end of the day. I also have a secondary list of items that need attention but not immediate. I'll check off what I can and will carry over anything that doesn't get done. Sometimes those items get moved to the "three things".

How do you build relations with your employees?

I think we need to take the time to learn about them, their work persona and who they are outside of the office. Sometimes that's with a five-minute check in or with a scheduled feedback session or performance review. Knowing your boundaries in the process is crucial but taking the time to listen is imperative and can help you understand their motives. Also, being open to feedback from your staff is important. Knowing that there is always room for improvement within yourself and being ok with hearing it. This takes effort and time but will pay off in dividends.

Three recurring challenges you face at your current position:

First, things are always changing. Rules, regulations, and processes are in a constant state of flux. This can create dissatisfaction and frustration in staff and helping them understand the "why" and giving them the proper tools to make the changes is crucial. Second, the "we've always done it this way" mentality. Leading others to change is challenging but necessary for growth. Knowing how particular staff will react and guiding them through the emotions of it will help to make the changes less painful for all involved. Third, staff turnover can create hostile feelings in veteran employees, especially for those who step into management positions. This is a tough one to work through and I don't think there's a magic bullet but it's taking the time to listen and hear their concerns, valid or not, is important. Then challenging them to think about a solution to their problem.

Three ways a potential leader can learn the ropes of rising to the top of your organization through service.

Challenge yourself to keep learning. Read books and articles about leadership and put their knowledge into practice. Know your strengths and weaknesses. Play to your strengths. Learn to see other's strengths and weaknesses and help them identify them and use them to be better staff and co-workers. Be willing to do the hard stuff, push yourself to be uncomfortable. Show others that you are willing to do so, set an example. Celebrate your wins but own up to your mistakes and use that to guide others.

What trends do you see in leadership?

I see understanding the generational differences and using that knowledge to break free from the norms and traditional work settings.

How can this trend be embedded into contemporary organizations for success?

I think we've already started since COVID. We've learned how to rethink where and how we work and were forced to be creative in serving our customers and staff, giving them a successful work environment outside of the traditional four walls, brick, and mortar offices. It has forced us to rethink how we interact with each other and with customers and given us the freedom to try new ways of communicating borne out of necessity. It has also given us the challenge of creating new processes and making them better, again, borne out of necessity as we learn to work remotely.

*Assessment: Reflect and summarize leadership ideas you picked from this interview. *

General Manager, Receiving Department of a Manufacturing Company.

For my personal experience as a leader at the receiving department of our organization throughout the years, I've found that having good relationships with each colleague or employee of yours makes it a lot easier to lead. When you don't have good relationships with your peers, it makes them more hesitant to put their trust in you. I do believe leaders should serve first. What makes a great/trustworthy leader is putting other people's needs before your own in your organization.

What motivated you into your current leadership position?

I began my career in this organization when I was 16 years old, after deciding that I did not want to attend college, I knew I wanted to climb the ladder within this company. When you don't have a degree to fall back on, it gives you an insane amount of drive to do well in each position you take on to grow within the company.

Walk me through how you plan for a typical day at work.

I usually get in at 7 a.m. before the majority of my employees arrive so I can get a few things done on my computer such as: sort our trucking routes, see what kind of meetings I have for that day, check everyone's hours, and make sure they are all on track, and check e-mails for any inquiries regarding product requests.

How do you build relations with your employees?

From the first day someone starts working for me, I like to be out on the floor with them and connect with them on a personal level. I typically ask questions about what they like to do for fun, what sports teams they like, etc., so we can develop a rapport.

Three recurring challenges you face at your current position.

Since most of my employees are college students, their schedules are always changing. Though we respect their school schedules, they often say they won't be in on a whim because of school meetings or assignments that come up. This can be frustrating on short notice because it leaves us short-handed. Also, most of our college student employees only want to work mornings, leaving us short staffed in the afternoons when we are the busiest. Again, as you can see, there is a trend happening here. Most of the challenges I deal with have to do with our employees that are students. None of them want to work Fridays.

How do you solve those challenges? What strategies do you use?

While I do want to respect the fact that the majority of the people, I hire are students, it can be incredibly frustrating to sometimes feel like they are taking advantage of the job just because they know I offer flexible hours. I expect the same respect I give them in return, and if I feel that is being abused, I usually have a sit-down talk with them to let them know I am unimpressed with the work being shown.

Recommend three ways a potential leader can learn the ropes of rising to the top of your organization through service.

First, try out many different positions within the organization to exercise your knowledge in all facets of the company. Second, form good relationships with higher ups, show them you are serious about wanting to further your career within the organization, ask them for feedback and always lend a helping hand. Third, be patient. If you have a goal of rising to the very top, it's not going to happen overnight. Try applying for many different positions and take every day as a learning experience.

What trends do you see in the future of leadership?

A trend I would like to see in the future is encouraging employees to explore other career opportunities within an organization after a certain period of time within a certain department. I have seen managers shame employees for wanting to grow within organizations and I think instead they should be applauded for wanting to branch out.

How can this trend you mentioned be embedded into contemporary organizations for success?

It would be beneficial because employees who have experience in multiple different departments might offer a bit more knowledge or input on company matters than someone who doesn't have such experience.

*Assessment: Reflect and summarize leadership ideas you picked from this interview. *

Lead Researcher at a Major University

I define leadership as the compilation and management of people's ideas and workflows. Leader should lead first but should have a willingness to follow. A belief in natural leadership skills and common sense as well as being competent at job and an interest in people and their job motivated me into leadership.

Walk me through how you plan for a typical day at work.

I plan a week in advance; come in an hour early, dedicate time to checking in on employees, putting higher priority to longer tasks than shorter ones.

How do you build relations with your employees?

Good communication, frequently checking in with them, having no agenda when talking with them.

Recommend three ways a potential leader can learn the ropes of rising to the top of your organization through service.

Be on good terms with everyone both higher and lower positions; work hard on a daily basis and get exposure to different leadership styles through training and development.

Three recurring challenges you face at your current position.

People good at helping but forget daily duties, employees keeping normal work hours, and being undermined sometimes because of my gender. Sometimes, some of my male colleagues do not take me seriously and I feel my gender has something to do with it.

How do you solve those challenges? What strategies do you use?

Sign off sheet for day-to-day responsibilities. I also set expectation, disciplinary hearings that are filed and act as a strike system. Moreover, I reassert opinion firmly yet politely, showing good judgment as a leader and using workplace relationships to reinforce authority.

What trends do you see in the future of leadership?

Communication on multiple platforms, adaptable leadership, virtualization of work, and technological personality matching for jobs.

How can this trend you mentioned be embedded into contemporary organizations for success?

Literacy in conference calls, virtual competence, practicing skills to be better than the average employee, and dedicated training sessions.

*Assessment: Reflect on ideas of this interview and share insights you gained from the responses.

Aerospace Engineers

How do you define leadership from your personal experience as a leader?

Interviewee One: A leader is someone who gives their team the necessary tools to be successful, allowing the group to meet or exceed expectations. This can come in many forms including data, reports, training opportunities, exposure to various levels of the organization, etc.

Interviewee Two: Leadership defined from my point of view is not just being there and making decisions for the business. But being there for people to work with the business. Knowing what can be done with them, where they can go, what they can do. Making decisions that some might not like but making them to help the company to make sure the customer is satisfied.

Interviewee Three: A guided decision maker or someone who takes all the information in and can make an educated decision to successfully enhance a person, group, or idea. They have a solution to any problem whether it is right or wrong, it's a step toward the overall goal.

Do you believe leaders must serve first? Why or why not?

Interviewee One: Yes, I've found that serving your team members leads to greater buy-in to goals and a greater willingness of people to go above and beyond to help others. It has only helped when team members see you doing the same things.

Interviewee Two: Yes, I believe to be a true leader, one must do this to show people that they are not just there for the company but to make sure they know that the employees' matter.

Interviewee Three: Yes and no, every day I see leaders or people in a position to be a leader not understanding simple basics of how things function, and I believe you need at least the minimal understanding of something to make an educated decision otherwise, you're being setup for failure. On the other hand, you need to trust in the experts you work with to help direct you into a decision.

What motivated you into your current leadership position?

Interviewee One: I've always enjoyed being in a leadership position whether it be sports or business. I enjoy helping others develop and attain goals they otherwise thought might not be possible. I've also always wanted to be in a position to where I'm significantly impacting the overall business whether it be making decisions or offering data driven suggestions.

Interviewee Two: What motivated me into the role was me wanting to move up in the business. Wanting to learn as much as I can and wanting to show that I can take on any task.

Interviewee Three: The opportunity to see something grow to better the business and the way we do things.

Walk me through how you plan for a typical day at work.

Interviewee One: Each afternoon I take some time looking at my "to do" list and set a goal on what I need and want to accomplish for the next day.

Interviewee Two: First thing in the day is finding out who is there or on vacation. Then is waiting to see if anyone calls in. Know the skill set of available people for work. Know what is due and form what cell. Know where help may be needed. Assign available people for work demand and move when needed. I also always try to plan for the next day if I am able to.

Interviewee Three: My drive to work and the drive home the day before and the sleepless nights I spend thinking of ways I need to make my area more efficient and cost effective by attacking the low hanging fruit first. By the time I get to work most of that all goes out the window because of fires that need to be put out on the shop floor.

How do you build relations with your employees?

Interviewee One: I try to ensure I'm recognizing and am providing positive feedback when my team members do something above & beyond or attain a goal. On the other end, I also try to be open with feedback when it comes to constructive criticism. I find that people want to know when something needs to be corrected. Also, I like to show interest in what people have going on outside of work.

Interviewee Two: Talking, showing, and telling them about yourself and asking if they want to do the same. Getting to know them and if they want or can do more, any idea will help. Be a leader, but also be a normal person.

Interviewee Three: Get your hands dirty and work side by side to fully understand how things affect a person's work life physically and mentally. Listen and build off their ideas.

Three recurring challenges you face at your current position.

Interviewee One: Backfilling lost staff and having the ability to succession plan; finding & utilizing the necessary tools to pull data from, and getting all the functions in the organization to the table to prioritize and make decisions on critical issues

Interviewee Two: Knowing when people can do more but choose not to; emotions, knowing when to push or just be nice. Not all people handle their emotions the same, you need to find that balance. Understanding how to motivate certain individuals.

Interviewee Three: Shrinking workforce; automation and decreasing process cost.

How do you solve those challenges? What strategies do you use?

Interviewee One: Utilize the creation of unique trainee positions to help on the succession side. For backfilling, I just try to stay in communication with HR and keep a rolling count of positions so we can show any losses over time.

Interviewee Two: With motivating, that relies on you and them, some do not want to be motivated and just are there for a paycheck. Others want to do this and just need guidance and be shown and told that they do have a voice and can use it. Leadership training and guidance from peers and mentors, having go to people that have experience with issues and advice to help you. Trial and error. Everything still is a learning experience, and I will not always get it right, but knowing and learning form it is key.

Interviewee Three: With a shrinking workforce I need to incorporate more automation to replace process jobs. This gives opportunity to decrease the labor cost but leads to a long period on my return on investment (ROI). Strategies use are to break processes down to its simplest form to make a step by step process a machine or robot may be able to accomplish.

Three ways a potential leader can learn the ropes of rising to the top of your organization through service.

Interviewee One: Adapt your approach to people based on their personality and their needs. I've found EI to be a much bigger indicator of success than IQ. Show ambition and be willing to take things on that you otherwise may not have. This shows leadership that you're wanting to grow and improve. It can lead to various networking and relationships as you're working through projects/opportunities. And it can also lead to exposure to higher levels in the organization. Involve others where possible. Show interest in opportunities throughout the organization.

Interviewee Two: Be role models. Ask for feedback. Do not be afraid to expand you network, people.

Interviewee Three: Watch everything leaders do. Attitude, reactions, thought process, decision and how they affect the company goal. Ask questions and analysis the answers. Listen and learn. Learn something from every problem and encounter. Educate yourself to understand how things work.

What trends do you see in the future of leadership?

Interviewee One: In the current environment and what I suspect will continue at a lot of organizations, virtual leadership. Leaders will have to adapt to not being at a location with employees but rather have employees working from home. I also have seen leaders that I've worked with adapt more to a serve first style. I think that leadership across businesses will be getting younger with many of the current generation leaders nearing retirement.

Interviewee Two: Being there for people, working with them and not being afraid to do the same. Education helps, always learn as much as you can. Never be afraid to ask for help or guidance. Trial and Error. Some of the best lessons are from mistakes. No one is perfect, and it is a losing battle to try to be.

Interviewee Three: Lack of attachment. More off hand management resulting in poor decisions, and lack of understanding and missing opportunities.

Fitness Manager and a Pastor

Interviewee One is a Fitness Manager. This manager is also a top Personal Trainer & Bodybuilding Coach with over 200 Clients, who pays over $1,000 a Month. **Interviewee Two** has been a Pastor for 40 years with over 2000 church members.

Defining Leadership.

Interviewee One: The ability to influence through modeling and teaching such that autonomy is gained. Leaders must serve first. They must continue to serve as it's a component of integrity.

Interviewee Two: Step-forward in every area that needs to be covered. Ask your followers, what do they need from you? Leaders must be ready to serve first. That is what you are called to do. Christ came to serve us.

What Motivated You into Your Current Leadership Position?

Interviewee One: Leadership is about teaching. The route of teaching begins with learning. I am extremely passionate about learning and learning for a lifetime. A component of learning is teaching and vice versa.

Interviewee Two: When I was three- years old, I knew I wanted to be a pastor. I looked up to my pastor at the time. He was one of my role models and I knew I wanted to follow in his footsteps.

Walk Me Through Your Typical Day at Work.

Interviewee One: My schedule is very consistent. Starting the day with meditation and self-care. Then 8 -10 hours of in person clients at the gym. Then 2–3 hours of building client programs. Fridays are online client check-ins, which takes up 10 to 12 hours."

Interviewee Two: My days are full of research for the Sunday sermon. I try to write them not for myself, but for what my congregations need to hear that week.

How Do You Build Relations with Your Employees?

Interviewee One: For me this would be building relationships with clientele. The center of this revolves around communication. The better the communication, the better the relationship.

Interviewee Two: Personal contact. This can be done by greeting people at the door before church begins or doing random home visits.

Three Recurring Challenges You Face as A Leader.

Interviewee One: Client adherence to their plan, time management and self-care. My time is predominantly business and client focused. The other one is communication. There is always lack of results due to clients not communicating with me sufficiently.

Interviewee Two: People, People and People! Every day, there are constant struggles with members of the church. This could range from an absent member to a grieving member of the church that just lost a loved one.

Solving Those Challenges. What Strategies Do You Use?

Interviewee One: I know that it seems ambiguous but in reality, this would look very different for each individual organization. In my case, creating better ways for my clients to track their diet, communicate freely with me, and have built in accountability has improved my business and success with clients.

Interviewee Two: I believe the answer here is prayer. Lots and lots of prayer. There are some problems that manmade strategies cannot solve except prayers.

Recommend Different Ways A Potential Leader Can Learn the Ropes of Rising the Top of Your Organization.

Interviewee One: Spend time in their "shoes". I learn how to do each task with mastery, even the smallest ones, and I am patient with the process.

Interviewee Two: Take it to the Lord in prayer; make good use of technology and be open to criticism.

What Trends Do You See in The Future of Leadership?

Interviewee One: If 2020 has taught us anything, it's that being adaptable is an integral attribute. As a leader, moving forward, I think it's even more important to be cognizant and resilient of being adaptable.

Interviewee Two: I see technology continuing to boom. Especially with our church services moving to Zoom video calls.

How this Trend you mentioned can be embedded into your organization for Success?

Interviewee One: Many long tenured leaders have not had to or resisted the learning curve of evolving technology. Thus, the openness, and one could say adaptability to learning new technology as it evolves could be a crucial aspect to continue to successfully lead.

Interviewee Two: I believe it is super important to always have your sources cited and have accurate information. You never know what websites and articles can be fake.

Summary of Thoughts

Judging from all interviewees' responses, it is clear that most of them have been practicing servant leadership yet, they don't know. This is how learning occurs. There are many things we do without knowing the technical names for it. If most leaders will practice these narrated stories at the workplace, toxicity will be a thing of the past. A leader who inspires and engage others to achieve a common good for an organization or community is a servant leader. Such a leader leads an exemplary live; models the way, builds a healthier team, shapes curious brains, allow employees to dream and create co-servants. Robert Greenleaf is the father of Servant Leadership, the same way as Adam Smith is the father of economics or Frederick Taylor the father of scientific management. Greenleaf defined servant leadership as serving first. and through conscious efforts, become the leader.

CHAPTER 9

Servant Leadership and The Religious Environment

"The misuse of creation begins when we no longer recognize any higher instance than ourselves,
when we see nothing else but ourselves." Pope Benedict XVI, 2008, p. 634.

Servant leaders have confidence in who they are and what is in their head. They are empathetic with vision and mission. According to Robert Greenleaf, seminaries are best positioned in the structure of our society to inspirit the churches and equip them with the prophetic vision to become a forceful society-building influence (1996). The church is the natural arena to live out servant leadership principles. In today's church, the pastor's role consists of two sides: spiritual and managerial. A servant leader will succeed at both sides if properly trained, principles practiced, and proper tone set within a congregation. The challenge today is that many pastors are not prepared to handle the 'people' side of ministry- change, conflict, and volunteer management.

It is out of this desire to serve one another that the servant leader is born. Jesus Christ served as an ultimate example of a servant leader. To love is to serve (Jones, 1995, p.251) He had a plan. He had a team. He did the difficult things. He prized the seed rather than the banquet. He had a passionate commitment to the cause. He gave them a vision greater than themselves. He served them. Being a servant leader also meant active listening, being self-aware, being respectful, being a change agent, and being a manager of conflict. Servant leaders are intentional in their work. They plan for crucial conversations when needed. Servant leaders lift up others to engage their gifts and form more servant leaders in the process. These skill sets cannot be learned solely from a book. They must be practiced daily. They must be lived.

The Church and Environmental Issues.

By connecting theological social statements and servant leadership principles, individuals enlarge their vision of stewardship, create supportive relationships with each other and with the natural environment surrounding their church. The question that pops up is, how do religious institutions determine their response to environmental issues and what do they see as their call to care for creation? Undoubtedly, there are multiple answers to this question. Many theological institutions have formal position statements on environmental support or caring for creation.

Humanity is intimately related to the rest of creation. We, like other creatures, are formed from the earth (Genesis 2:7,9,19). Scripture speaks of humanity's kinship with other creatures (Psalm 104, Job 38-39).

Humans, in service to God, have special roles on behalf of the whole of creation. Made in the image of God, we are called to care for the earth as God cares for the earth. God's command to have dominion and subdue the earth is not a license to dominate and exploit. Human dominion (Genesis 1:28: Psalm 8), a special responsibility, should reflect God's way of ruling as a shepherd king who takes the form of a servant (Philippians 2:7), wearing a crown of thorns" (pp. 2-3).

Catholicism and the Environment.

The Catholic church has provided guiding documents for the actions they believe are necessary to support the environment. In his encyclical letter, *Laudato Si'*, (2015), *On Care for Our Common Home*, Pope Francis reminds the reader "this sister (Mother Earth) cries out to us because of the harm we have inflicted on her by our irresponsible use and abuse of the goods with which God has endowed her…the violence present in our hearts, wounded by sin, is also reflected in the symptoms of sickness evident in the soil, in the water, in the air and in all forms of life"(p. 1). His predecessors, Pope Paul VI (1971) and Saint John Paul II (1979) and Pope Benedict XVI (2008) similarly expressed overwhelming concern towards the abuse of creation in prior publications and "where everything is simply our property, and we use it for ourselves alone.

Pope Francis (2015) addressed the interconnectedness of all of creation and the ramifications of the loss of biodiversity. When speaking of the short-sighted approaches to economic situations, he postulates that the earth and all of the inhabitants are or will be paying a heavy price in the future. His argument also extends to not just human suffering and loss, but calls forward theological implications that "because of us, thousands of species (are becoming extinct) and no longer give glory to God by their very existence, nor convey their message to us. We have no such right" (p. 9). The encyclicals also speak to the relationship between faith and the duty Christians have towards nature and our fellow travelers. "It is good for humanity and the world at large when we believers better recognize the ecological commitments which stem from our convictions" (p. 17).

Native Christianity.

According to Josiah Baker, (2016) the Native Christian religious identity is very special-centric. "Ethical decisions are concerned with one's relation to creation and one's tribe; spiritual practices are drawn from the environment of the tribal community, and conceptions of communal and individual identity are entirely focused on surroundings" (p. 235). Baker contrasts traditional European Christianity, which would typically use a timeline of events such as the creation, the fall, the crucifixion and the resurrection to describe their faith, with the Native Traditionalists' use of place as the cornerstone of their faith: sacred mountains, ritual locations, etc. (p. 236).

Another significant theological viewpoint that may shape the Native Christian attitude toward the environment is their understanding of the kingdom of God. Baker (2016) states that European Christians typically discuss the kingdom of God in reference to "when" while the Native Christian would suggest that the more accurate question would be "where" is the kingdom of God. They would suggest that it is now present and furthermore, present everywhere, because God is omnipresent in all of creation. Consequently, if God is present in all of creation, humans are called to return to a right relationship of mutual care with all of creation "It is a Christian imperative to strive for peace in every place throughout creation" (pp. 238-239).

In addition to the previously mentioned thoughts, Josiah Baker (2016) discusses the relationship between Native Christianity, Covenant Theology and Liberation Theology as it pertains to respecting, nurturing and liberating all of creation from broken relationships and covenants. When coupled with the previously discussed strong belief in what is referred to in Baker's writing as Placement Theology, the idea of caring for creation within Native Christianity assumes primary importance (pp. 243-244).

Priestly Function Philosophy.

Norman Wirzba (2011) in *A Priestly Approach to Environmental Theology: Learning to Receive and Give Again the Gifts of Creation,* presents what is typically considered an Orthodox theology toward the environment. By discussing the priestly functions of asceticism, sacrifice and gratitude in relationship to creation as a type of "good shepherding…that provides an opportunity to exercise and refine skill in the arts of care, patience, intelligence, affection, and land management" (p. 355), the author posits that through these behaviors we will be more able to live honestly and humbly as one part of God's creation (p. 361).

Mission Theology.

Historically, mission or outreach has been a significant focus of many Christian denominations. Typically, this has referred to a type of evangelism that consists of spreading the gospel to various groups, or what is known as the Great Commission:

[16] Now the eleven disciples went to Galilee, to the mountain to which Jesus had directed them. [17] And when they saw him, they worshiped him, but some doubted. [18] And Jesus came and said to them, "All authority in heaven and on earth has been given to me. [19] Go therefore and make disciples of all nations, baptizing them in the name of the Father and of the Son and of the Holy Spirit, [20] teaching them to observe all that I have commanded you. And behold, I am with you always, to the end of the age" Matthew 28:16-20 English Standard Version (ESV).

In the article, *Christian Mission and Environmental Issues: An Evangelical Reflection,* Rev. Dave Bookless (2008) states it is his belief that this view of mission is too anthropocentric and fails to examine mission attitudes, values, and their ensuing behaviors toward creation. This author references two prominent modern-day theologians, N.T. Wright (1994) and David Bebbington (1989), as a way to broaden the concept of mission to "include not just people but also the non-human creation, not merely preparing for heaven but also caring for earth" (Bookless, 2008, p. 38). While each of the above-mentioned authors has a unique outline with which to view biblical history, the gospel and mission, Bookless (2008) successfully juxtaposed these two frameworks to make his argument that they both point to the significance of God's saving plan for creation and the role humans play within that plan. He concludes by emphatically stating that Christian communities have a Biblical moral imperative to advocate and work for sustainability, globally and locally, as well as challenge western materialism as a driver of ecological devastation (pp. 47-50). The way forward is for the church to have a very active social ministry and outward facing mission focus. A Green Team needs to be developed with a setup of a Social Ministry Committee to take care of the environmental issues. The idea of creation care as a type of mission experience must be an overt discussion within the group. Would this mission focus increase the enthusiasm for and viability of environmental projects? This was identified as a potential area of future research.

Determinants of Environmental Action

Research has shown that formal theological statements are not the sole driver or determinants of action among faith communities. Arbuckle and Konisky (2015) in the book, *The Role of Religion in Environmental Attitudes,* analyzed and cited previous studies that would indicate that there is less concern for environmental issues among those denominations that are considered fundamental Christians (Boyd, 1999; Eckberg & Blocker, 1989; Woodrum & Hoban, 1994). Although previously stating that the evidence was weak and somewhat inconclusive, their detailed study analysis led them to conclude that "people affiliating with Judeo-Christian traditions tend to express weaker environmental attitudes than individuals who do not affiliate with an established denomination" (Arbuckle and Konisky, 2015, p. 1259) and also that a higher level of religiosity and literalism had a negative correlation to environmental concerns. They believe this provides partial support for Lynn White's early and controversial publication entitled, *The Historical Roots of Our Ecological Crisis,* in which he blames a perceived Christian philosophy of dominion over nature as the cause of a careless and exploitative view of creation (White, 1967).

In their study review, Arbuckle and Konisky (2015) found political ideology, rather than theological beliefs, to be one of the biggest predictors of environmental behavior. This same finding was supported by Severson and Coleman (2015) in their article, *Moral Frames and Climate Change Policy Attitudes.* These authors studied two population groups (conservatives and liberals) and six possible determinants of environmental actions. These determinants included the following: positively framed arguments about the scientific consequence of climate change, negatively framed arguments about the scientific consequence of climate change, religious-deontological moral framed arguments about climate change, secular-deontological moral framed arguments about climate change, economic-efficiency framed arguments about the scientific consequence of climate change, economic-equity framed arguments about the scientific consequence of climate change, and finally, a control condition receiving no frame.

Their findings, as related to political ideology, were fascinating as well as intriguing. As stated in the previously cited article written by Arbuckle and Konisky (2015), a religious-deontological moral framework did not increase the probability of environmentally protective behaviors. Only by utilizing positively framed messages about climate change actions and economic equity framed messages was the effect of political partisanship or ideology reduced (Severson & Coleman, 2015, p.1287). If individuals are truly motivated information processors as suggested by David Redlawsk (2002) in *"Hot Cognition or Cool Consideration? Testing the Effects of Motivated Reasoning on Political Decision Making"* how the information is presented may determine the potential opportunity for successful environmental project uptake.

Social capital such as generalized trust, or "the widespread trust in the integrity of others we may not even know" (Macias, 2015, p. 1274) was suggested to be another environmental behavior change motivator and a predictor of willingness to sacrifice through engagement in actions supporting the common good. Regarding environmental behaviors, generalized trust is based on the belief that positive actions and forms of self-sacrifice will not only be done by the person actively engaging in them but also by others as well. However, it was also recognized that certain populations may be hesitant to trust because of past environmental and social injustices (Macias, 2015). In response to this potential lack of generalized trust, Macias (2015) stated that "face-to-face interactions in diverse neighborhood settings appear to be an important predictor of this particular aspect of social capital among the poor and race and ethnic minorities in the United States and Canada" (Macias, 2015, p. 1265). This opinion was also supported by Marschall and Stolle, (2004) and Stolle, Soroka and Johnston, (2008).

Benefits of Religious Institutional Involvement with Environmental Efforts

Religious institutions can offer some unique benefits to the environmental movement. Although many for-profit agencies as well as non-profit organizations play a significant role in addressing environmental issues, Gary Gardner (2003) in his article, *Religion and the Quest for a Sustainable World,* states that religious organizations collectively have various significant assets that could provide a noteworthy positive environmental influence when utilized effectively. Firstly, religious institutions have the opportunity to influence the world view or cosmology of their members. Secondly, the church provides guidance for, and is frequently seen as, a moral authority for both individual and community behavior. Thirdly, organized religion, as a collective body of people, has a large base of adherents.

Over 80% of the world's population claim to belong to one of the world religions, giving them a very large audience for messaging. Fourthly, in addition to a large percentage of the population, religious institutions also reportedly own up to 7% of the world's habitable areas. If ecologically managed well, these lands could provide an increase in global environmental sustainability and a significant visual example of a supportive doctrine of caring for creation. Lastly, church affiliation provides opportunities for community building and a potential for high social capital when there are unifying causes. Bookless (2008) would also agree that churches have an opportunity to encourage an increased sense of personal well-being that is fostered by following a biblical imperative, supporting local and global eco-evangelism and engaging in community building.

Challenges of Religious Institutional Involvement with Environmental Efforts

Another study, by Jens Koehrsen (2015) describes some of those same assets but his research points to a different conclusion. Because of the highly partisan nature of the United States citizenry, he chose to carry out his research regarding the impact of religion on environmental changes in Emden, a city in north-western Germany. His findings would indicate that although the aforementioned assets may be a possibility, they did not affect change in Emden. His findings suggested that frequently church resources are limited and divided among numerous social and political justice issues. These conclusions were also supported by the work of Minton, Xie, Gurel-Atay and Kahle (2017). The focus of their research was the relationship between religion, sustainable consumption and subjective well-being. Although they offer a great deal of support for the role religion plays with positive subjective well-being, possibly because "sustainable consumption practices…may actually produce happiness, in part due to satisfaction in showing reverence to one's God(s)" (p. 661), they also concluded that there is a lack of research in this field, limiting the findings that could be reported confidently.

Mutual misperceptions between environmentalists and religion or people of faith was mentioned as another challenge in the reviewed articles. Gary Gardner, (2003) speculates that this "growing chasm between science and religion" (p. 12) could again stem from the frequently cited work by Lynn White that implicated the religious dominion theory as the cause of the climate crisis. Gardner also states that even if the above criticism of religious institutions is falsely based on an inaccurate and partial reading of White's essay, there are other areas that may lend themselves to a general mistrust of religion by environmentalists. He stated, "Where religions neglect their prophetic potential and their calling to be critics of immoral social and environmental realities, they are likely to be distrusted by those working to change those trends" (p.12). Similarly, these two groups may hold differing opinions or worldviews on other sensitive issues such as women's rights that causes an alienation between the two groups leading to a generalized animosity (Gardner, 2003).

Green Space Creation and Community Benefits.

Several arguments in support of green space development would include not only environmental benefits, but also health and social benefits to a variety of age groups and backgrounds (Kingsley, 2019; Louv, 2011; and Balls-Berry, 2018). Kingsley (2019) calls forward the significant potential benefits of even limited green space to those populations that may not otherwise have access to them. These co-benefits of green space existence were also supported by previous authors suggesting that those groups who are most vulnerable, either because of low income, racialization or ages on the upper or lower end of the continuum, seem to derive the greatest benefits from the availability of green space (Mitchell, 2008). In particular, the health of children has been shown to be positively impacted when well-maintained parks with playgrounds are in close proximity to their residence (Potwarka, 2008). The health of vulnerable groups has been shown to experience the benefits of green space even with a fairly small increase in nearby green space density (Mitchell, 2015).

In his book, *The Nature Principle,* Richard Louv (2011) states one of his primary assertions is that "reconnecting to nature is one key to growing a larger environmental movement" (p. 284). If the desire is to protect the environment, it is important to experience the power and wonder of nature. Throughout his book, Louv (2011) immerses the chapters with countless reasons and substantial rationale for a return to getting dirty and spending time outside,

not just to receive the personal benefits but also to form relationships with the other creature inhabitants of the world. His message is one of warning related to inactivity but also hope as he references a growing international movement towards renaturing neighborhoods and the awareness that this must be a right for people of all economic levels.

Physical Amenity Considerations in Green Space Development

When reviewing green space utilization within a subset of existing faith communities, Susan Bratton (2012) in *The Megachurch in the Landscape: Adapting to Changing Sale and Managing Integrated Green Space in Texas and Oklahoma, USA,* posited the following "five theological questions religious campus planners (should) include regarding the role of green space. How does this green space: 1) express God's beauty? 2) honor providential environmental services? 3) teach about the relationship between God, humanity, and the environment? 4) provide connections among God, nature, the congregations, and the neighbors? and 5) provide for the needs of others? (p. 47).

In her review, Bratton (2012) found a significant variation between the megachurches that she analyzed. Some of the churches had very private space design, while others were more easily accessible to the public. Also, religious symbols were prominently displayed in some green spaces while other churches chose to keep any Christian symbolism to a minimum, believing that it would be more welcoming to the non-churched or those with past negative experiences within a church environment. The consistent theme noted in her article, however, was that "for large congregations, green space remains an underutilized resource" (p. 30).

Another study completed in Sweden looked at the relationship between perceived monetary value related to the various characteristics and multifunctionality of urban green spaces (Czembrowski, et. al.,2019). This was a helpful perspective because of the previously cited study that references economic-efficiency as one of the motivational factors for green space conversion. In this article, the authors create a "hedonic pricing study based on two stages: the ranking of five general characteristics of urban green spaces according to monetary value and…secondly to estimate the monetary value of the multifunctionality of green spaces" (p. 2). They concluded the green space characteristics were valued in the following order from most highly valued to most unfavorable: aesthetic quality, social opportunities, nature attribute, physical activity options, and finally play and recreation equipment (p. 11).

Utilizing Servant Leadership Principles in the Green Space Conversion Process.

Jeff Thompson (2017), in his book, Lead True, makes the following statement, "If you don't have the courage to implement your values, then they are just words (p. 33). Similarly, Izzo and Vanderwielen (2018) in the Purpose Revolution, make a very compelling argument for the need to "clearly find and name your purpose. Once you have named it your job is to move it to center stage. By that we mean you must live the purpose you profess" (p. 35). Izzo and Vanderwielen (2018) go on to state that "leadership is personal, emerging from your heart, transcendent, altruistic and forward thinking" (p. 105). These thoughts were compelling motivators for action on this author's personal value of environmental stewardship.

Robert Greenleaf (2008), in The Servant as Leader, states that "Everything begins with the initiative of an individual" and also that "every achievement starts with a goal…the one who states the goal must elicit trust, especially if it is a high risk or visionary goal, because those who follow are asked to accept the risk along with the leader" (pp. 16-17). Greenleaf (2008) also states that one cannot lead if no one chooses to follow. He emphasizes the role of power and authority within servant leadership and that people will only freely chose to follow leaders who are seen and trusted to be servants (p.12). Another one of the characteristics of a servant leader that is cited by Robert Greenleaf (2008) is the ability to listen and understand. True listening by a leader builds strength in other people. If the church leaders will listen, we will save the environment and have great relations with nature for our own sustenance.

CHAPTER 10
Servant Leadership and Wisdom

"Wisdom and goodness are twin-born, one heart must hold both sisters, never seen apart."
– William Cowper, English Poet and Hymnodist, Expostulations, 1, 634, 1782.

We often differentiate between wisdom and knowledge. The latter is something we acquire through intelligence and learning. Wisdom, on the other hand, doesn't necessarily result from a high intelligent quotient (IQ). We've all known people of extraordinary intelligence who weren't very bright when it comes to everyday good judgment. King Solomon had both knowledge and wisdom. Wisdom is a highly prized gift from the creator. Michael Fox, in a commentary on proverbs points out that the Hebrew translation of wisdom is *hokmah*, which is a combination of theoretical learning and practical skills. He suggests that the best English equivalent is the word "expertise." The scientific method helps to control variables that may skew or hide a relationship of cause and effect, and this calls for wisdom to interpret and make the right decision.

As an example, if one even invariably follows another, when all other variables have been controlled, and if the other two possible relationships have been ruled out, then there is a probability of a cause-and-effect link. We can comfortably call this knowledge because there is sufficient warrant to back such a conclusion. In wisdom, we deal not in knowledge alone, but divine understanding and awareness in creating a virtuous experience. We are drowning in information but starving in wisdom in most cases. There is also abundance of opinions, but sometimes, lacks truth and discerning. That is when wisdom comes handy. Wisdom is seen from different perspectives.

These includes Judio-Christian, Philosophical, psychological, leadership and scientific. In a Scientific Study of wisdom from contemplative traditions to Neuroscience, Ferrari & Weststrate (2013) found that there are different ways and perspectives of wisdom, including decision making abilities, self-transcendent insight, pragmatically relevant insight, set of wisdom traits through personal characteristics, eloquence, social phenomenon, narrative process, and a combination of viewpoints. Therefore, wisdom could be culturally based. What is clear is that wisdom entails knowledge, experience, and virtue (Ludden, 2009, Sternberg, 2002; Sternberg, 2008).

Wisdom is related to intelligence, but they are contextually different in situational applications. Wisdom is special because it is oriented to maximize the common good of society, not for individual well-being. Sternberg (1885) proposed a Triarchic Theory of Intelligence. Triarchic comes from the word "Three." Do you remember your "Triangle"? The triarchic theory of intelligence are: Analytical, Creative and Practical. Analytically, intelligent individuals internally process skills and ideas to guide intelligent behavior. The creative piece of the triarchic involves ability to create optimal match between one's skills and their external environment, while the practical part is ability to capitalize on one's experiences to process both novel and unfamiliar information.

Developing from the triarchic theory of intelligence, Sternberg (1998) argued that tacit knowledge (practical intelligence), a component of practical intelligence, is a core feature of wisdom. Thus, Sternberg (1998) theorized wisdom as practical intelligence applied to maximize a balance of intrapersonal (various self-interest), interpersonal (interest of others) and other aspects of context in which one lives (Extrapersonal). Don't ever forget that balance is key in wisdom. Thus, a comprehensive definition of wisdom from Sternberg is below:

Wisdom is the application of tacit knowledge as mediated by values toward the achievement of a common good through a balance among multiple intrapersonal, interpersonal, and extrapersonal interests in order to achieve a balance among adaptation to existing environments, shaping of existing environments and selection of new environments (Sternberg, 1998, p. 347).

The by-product of this triarchic theory was *The Imbalance Theory of Foolishness.* Sternberg (2002) argued that smart people are not stupid, but they sure can be foolish. He considered foolishness as the extreme failure of wisdom. He contended that foolishness is the opposite of wisdom, and that, most behaviors referred to as stupid are not stupid as opposed to intelligence, but foolish as opposed to being wise. He then defined foolishness as:

Foolishness is the faulty acquisition or application of tacit knowledge as guided by values away from the achievement of a common good, through a balance among intrapersonal, interpersonal and extrapersonal interest of the short and long term, in order to achieve a balance among adaptation to existing environments, shaping of existing environments, and selection of new environments (Sternberg, 2002, p. 236.)

Sternberg believes foolishness results from individuals letting down their guard as a result of feelings of omniscience, omnipotence, and invulnerability. There have been different perspectives in learning wisdom from faith, philosophical, psychological to leadership perspective.

Judeo-Christian Perspective of Wisdom.

The fear of the Lord is the beginning of wisdom and knowledge of the Holy One is understanding (Proverbs 9:10). According to Lambert (2009) "To fear God is to nurture an attitude of awe and humility before Him and to walk in radical dependence upon God in each area of life. Wisdom, then, relates to trust, humility, teachability, servanthood, responsiveness, and reliance on God; it is the exact opposite of autonomy and arrogance (Ludden, 2013). In a related wisdom study, Hill, and Walton (1991) posited that to fear God entails the following seven (7) constructs:

1. Arises from a choice grounded in the human will.
2. Elicits genuine worship—willing obedience to his commands.
3. Dread at God's holiness & trepidation of divine judgment.
4. Faith and trust in God's plan for human life
5. Hating and avoiding evil and refusing to envy sinners.
6. Generally, reward of prosperity and long life.
7. Disciplined instruction that instills wisdom, humility, and honor.

Philosophical Perspective of Wisdom.

Early Greek philosophers, Socrates, Plato, & Aristotle Perceived wisdom as knowledge of the ideal or divine. They treated wisdom as a virtue that must be acted out. They also considered the contrast between contemplative, idealistic, or theoretical wisdom versus practical wisdom or prudence (Ludden, 2013).

Wisdom Wanes After the Enlightenment.

According to Whence, Whither, Rooney and McKenna (2007) the combined effects of the Renaissance, Scientific and Industrial Revolutions might have produced epistemological and axiological changes that facilitated contemporary business discourse and practice. Whence et al. (2007) posits that it seems to show that the rationalist principles of the modern scientific tradition valorized the rational processes of the mind and distrusted the role of the body's instincts and feelings, which has been identified as crucial to wise practice.

In another study on knowledge and wisdom, a revolution for science and the humanities, Maxwell (2008) argued that it appears mainline philosophy is more appropriately classified with the natural and social sciences than with the humanities or liberal arts. This is because its fundamental interest has been in knowledge rather than wisdom, and its fundamental inclination has been to oppose established beliefs and practices and not only the beliefs and practices of the common, 'vulgar' folk, but those of its own predecessors.

Psychological Perspective of Wisdom.

In psychology, researchers such as Yung, Ardelt and Erikson defined wisdom from their own perspective. Generally, wisdom definitions in psychology fits into the different categories below:

- **Composite of Characteristics or Competences.** Monika Ardelt (2003) defines wisdom as a personality characteristic that integrates cognitive, reflective, and affective personality qualities.
- **Positive Result of Human Development.** Erikson (1959) defines wisdom as the "ego strength" or virtue which emerges after a lifetime's resolution of psychosocial tensions and is manifested in a person's informed yet detached concern with life when facing death.
- **Collective System about the Meaning of Life.** According to Baltes and Kunzmann (2003), wisdom consists of:
  i. Rich factual knowledge about life and lifespan development.
  ii. Rich procedural knowledge about dealing with life problems.
  iii. Rich knowledge about the contexts of life and their dynamics.
  iv. Rich knowledge about the relativism of values and life goals.
  v. Recognition and management of uncertainty.

Leadership Perspective.

Sternberg (2002) defined wisdom as "the application of intelligence and creativity as mediated by values toward the achievement of a common good through a balance among: (a) Intrapersonal interests (b) Interpersonal interests, and (c) Extrapersonal interests.

Over the short- term and long-terms, in order to achieve a balance among:

a. adaptation to existing environments
b. shaping of existing environments, and
c. selection of new environments.

In a process view of wisdom study, Yang (2008) found a difference between personal and general wisdom. He stated that personal wisdom comes from individual's insights into their selves, their own lives. General wisdom, on the other hand, is insights into life in general from an objective point of view.

In another wisdom model development and study, Ludden (2009) defined Wisdom as a dynamic process a leader uses to apply knowledge, experience, and virtue in seeking truth that subsequently governs the leader's actions and decisions for the organization. He argued that wisdom engages a person's cognitive, affective, and conative abilities for personal, interpersonal, community, societal, and global improvement. Ludden further posited that Wisdom is manifested by continuously seeking more knowledge, experience, and virtuosity to achieve these ends. Imbibed in Ludden (2013) wisdom model are critical thinking and reflection. He stated:

Wisdom involves improving your thought processes and primary among these are critical thinking and reflection. In many ways, there is an iterative relationship between deep reflection about past experiences and understanding yourself while using critical thinking to understand, apply, analyze, synthesize, evaluate, and create knowledge.

Thus, the accumulation of wisdom fundamentally takes place through the acquisition of knowledge balanced with experience. The accumulation occurs through time but more importantly by strategically positioning oneself to obtain both knowledge and experience that meaningful increases a person's wisdom. In a follow-up study, Ludden (2013) found that Psychological wisdom research since 1970 has focused on: (a) Providing a lay definition of wisdom, (b) Conceptualizing and measuring wisdom, (c) Understanding and developing wisdom, (d) Investigating the plasticity of wisdom, (e) Applying psychological knowledge about wisdom to life contexts. Ludden further proposed best practices for applying wisdom: Think, Feel (emotive capacity), Synergize, Engage (behavioral proactiveness), Reflect and Aspire (extraordinary principled objectives).

In a related study, Rooney, McKenna and Routledge (2010) found that (a) Wisdom is based on reason and observation, (b) Wisdom incorporates non-rational and subjective elements into judgment, (c) Wisdom is directed to authentic humane and virtuous outcomes, (d) Wisdom is articulate, aesthetic, and intrinsically rewarding, and (e) Wisdom is practical. Kaipa and Radjou (2013), also theorized that wise leadership is leveraging smartness for the greater good by balancing action with reflection and introspection, gateways to humility and ethical clarity. From this perspective, they pointed out the following paradigms that show a leader's wisdom:

Perspective – influences & shapes worldview. Action Orientation – how a leader is driven to act. Role Clarity – choosing a role and identifying with it. Decision Logic – framework a leader uses to decide. Fortitude – determining when to hold and when to fold. Motivation – know what inspires and drives actions and decisions.

Hubert & Dreyfus (2001) also posited these stages of attaining wisdom: Novice – basic features of skill. Advanced Beginner – engage with real situations. Competent – plan and adapt as situations change. Proficiency – recognition of situations from past experience, pattern recognition. Expertise – differentiates situations into more finite classifications. Mastery – experiences times when performance transcends usual level of expertise. Practical Wisdom – connection of skill to culture and well-being of others. Meanwhile, Augustine's *Confessions Book VIII* portrayed wisdom as: Humility – fear of God. Piety – living out God's commands. Knowledge – makes hopeful not boastful. Fortitude – hunger and thirst for justice.

Misericordia – resolve of compassion. Purity of Heart – contemplate God with attitude of being dead to this world.

Finally, Ludden (2009) proposed principles of wisdom for leaders: (a) Wisdom is a quality leaders and organizations should strive to attain, (b) Wisdom is complex and requires effort to understand and develop, (c) Wisdom is not found in us but is from God and works through us, (d) Wisdom is a continuous process of searching and striving for truth, (e) Wisdom is to be pursued despite making foolish decisions, (f) Wisdom requires humility, inclusiveness, and vulnerability, and (g) Wisdom must become part of an organization's way of life.

Is Wisdom Teachable?

Wisdom is teachable only when we develop it first. Staudinger & Gluck (2011) hypothesized that General wisdom can be significantly increased by focusing on activities that develop wisdom-related capacity or processes. They argued that Personal wisdom can be improved when individuals are taught how to infer insight based on personal experiences. Based on these findings, Staudinger & Gluck (2011) concluded that Empirical studies provide evidence both general and personal wisdom can be facilitated. Robert Sternberg (2009) also proposed guidelines for teaching wisdom: (a) Emphasize dialogical & dialectical thinking in class activities, (b) Study truth and values developed during reflective thinking, (c) Emphasize critical, creative, and practical thinking in service of common good, (d) Think how ideas can be used for better or worse ends and how important the ends are, (e) Model wisdom by using Socratic method and encouraging students to play active role in constructing learning.

In another study on teaching personal wisdom, Ferrari (2008) found these activities to be effective: Reflect on one's own life experiences, discuss these reflections with a wise person, reflect on wisdom texts, engage in specific exercises that cultivate mindfulness, consider logical arguments that provoke a deeper understand of self, cultivate virtues, engage in social service, observation and evaluation of other people who are wise, apprentice with a wise person, and mentor other people to develop their wisdom.

CHAPTER 11
Servant Leadership and Executive Coaching

You get the best effort from others not by lighting a fire beneath them, but by building a fire within them. Bob Nelson.

Coaches push individuals to fly, not to drag them along. What is coaching then? It is a helping relationship formed between a client who has managerial authority and responsibility in an organization and a consultant who uses a wide variety of behavioral techniques and methods to help the client achieve a mutually identified set of goals to improve his or her professional performance and personal satisfaction and, consequently, to improve the effectiveness of the client's organization within a formally defined coaching agreement (Kilburg, 2000). Partnering with clients in a thought-provoking and creative process that inspires them to maximize their personal and professional potential (International Coach Federation, 2011). Improvement programs and major change initiatives seldom succeed without strong support by top management and middle management (Kotter, 2002). Executive coaching is different from coaching. Executive Coaching is a professional relationship between a qualified coach and an organization, individual or a team that supports the achievement of extraordinary results based on goals set by the organization, individual, or team.

Goals of Executive Coaching.

Be a catalyst for organizational change. Coaching is an intervention that has at its underlying and ever-present goal the building of others' self-belief, regardless of the content of the task or issue (Altman, 2007). Develop wise organizational leaders. The truly wise leaders are those who love what they do and pursue and practice them with temperance and courage (Kilburg, 2006). Unlocking a leaders' potential. Coaching is unlocking a person's potential to maximize their own performance. It is helping them to learn rather than teaching them (Gallwey,1974).

Coaches are utilized when: (a) something is at stake, (b) gap in knowledge, skills or behaviors, (c) need to create a more collaborative work environment, (d) style of relating is ineffective, (e) need for a course correction, (f) time management and organizational issues, (g) need to develop leadership presence, and (h) need to improve ability to develop others.

In a 2001 *Why Organizations Hire Outside Coaches'* survey of 1000 executives, the figures below were found:

#1 Reason (86%) – To develop the leadership talent of high potential individuals.

#2 Reason (72%) – To help a leader overcome a detrimental behavioral style/problem.

#3 Reason (64%) – To ensure the success of newly promoted managers.

#4 Reason (58%) – To develop the leadership and interpersonal skills of a leader with a strong artistic/ technical orientation

Source: Manchester Inc., January 2001, Impact Study of 1,000 Executives receiving coaching.

Benefits of Executive Coaching.

There are two major benefits of executive coaching: For Organizations, and For Executives.

A. For Organizations:

Accelerated goal attainment.

- Productivity enhancement.
- Improved relationships with direct reports, immediate supervisor, or team.
- Improved relationships cross-functionally.
- Increased leadership presence and confidence.

B. For Executives.

- Fresh perspectives and clarity.
- Enhanced thinking and decision-making skills.
- Accelerated achievement of goals.
- Increased confidence and productivity.
- Enhanced interpersonal skills.
- Increased influence.
- Ability to offer a perk.
- Increased leadership presence.

Schnell (2005) argued that during periods of exceptional demands, leaders are likely to feel unprepared, and coaching provides an opportunity for skill development that is directly linked to new actions needed to make the organization succeed. Most of the senior leader coaching ideas or areas of concentration are Vision, Values Clarification, Organizational Effectiveness survive, perform its mission, and maintain favorable earnings, financial resources, and asset value. Other areas include financial performance of an organizations, capital, Organizational Change, Facilitating Cultural Change, Staff Development, Skill Development (Conflict), Trust Behavior Change, and how top Executives influence financial performance and survival of organizations.

How Coaching Process Works.

a. Identifying and validate leader development need.

b. Document sponsor and high-level goals.

c. Discuss leader need with executive coaches.

d. Review coaching biographies provided by coaches.

e. Provide leader with coach biographies.

f. Leader and organization interview executive coaches.

g. Make executive coach selection

h. Sign 6-month agreement.

i. First meeting with sponsor, coach and individual.

j. Honor organizational check-in with sponsor and leader at 3 and 6-month point.

How Organizations Hire Coaches.

Organizations hire coaches for leadership development and transition support for new roles, global experience, to retain hi-performers, or for cross-cultural and cross-gender purposes.

Key factors in coaching success

Executive Coaching and Servant Leadership.

The establishment of trust is principle to developing a coaching culture of servant leadership; one in which the purpose for leading is to serve others through investment in their development and well-being (Page & Wong, 2000). Servant leadership is an actively implemented practice as a style of organizational management and proves to be one of the most ethical forms of leadership due to the multi-directional influence of interactions (Griffith, 2007). Servant leadership seeks to serve the highest needs of the people one leads by subjugating the needs of the leader to that of the follower (Greenleaf, 1977; Griffith, 2007). Organizations that show a culture rooted in servant leadership have success in employee engagement, interdependence, and meeting the needs of the employee (McGee & Trammell, 2013). This is achieved through several characteristics including: listening, empathy, healing, awareness, persuasion, conceptualization, foresight, stewardship, commitment to growth, and community building (Spears, 2010).

Coaching in the workplace also aims to reach the goals of the organization and focus on the professional development of an individual. Emerging coaching methods aim to offer a supportive environment for personal and professional development that values the inherent ability of an individual to find their own solutions (Forbes Coaches Council, 2018). It is an effort to serve the needs of the individual to reach their goals through supportive listening, understanding, awareness, learning and growth, and teamwork between participants. There is additional benefit in peer coaching because it eliminates the power dynamics commonly found in subordinate coaching (Parker & Carroll, 2009). If an organization can develop these values in coworker interactions, employee engagement and satisfaction may increase (Grant and Hartley, 2013).

Though servant leadership and coaching share some of the same goals, it is the method in which individuals interact that lead to their shared success. Coaching within the workplace may be a tool for effective leadership development and personal growth, for both the participant and coach. Many of the qualities of servant leadership can be argued to be found through effective coaching, but the characteristics of listening, empathy, awareness, commitment to growth, and community building are the primary focus of this study. Coaching in the workplace may develop positive interoffice relationships, build the qualities of servant leadership within an organization, and contribute to the personal and professional development of staff. There may be value in developing strong interpersonal relationships in the workplace through structured personal and professional developmental coaching sessions. Coaching is therefore, a structured (timed) session that is concentrated on the personal, professional, and individual goals of individuals, groups, or organizations.

Blanchard (1991) posited that people are looking beyond traditional models of management and there is a growing desire to have managers that are listeners, facilitators, and cheerleaders more than critics. The principles of servant leadership require an approach, where the servant leader wants to teach and coach individuals to achieve their goals and do their best. There is an understanding that people and process will always be more important than tasks and organizational structure in accomplishing goals. An important element of building a workplace rooted in servant leadership is not through strategy, but through culture. The qualities of servant leadership will be seen through the language of an organization to promote empowerment, shared vision, teamwork, and leaders that strive to be more consultative, relational, and self-effacing (Page & Wong, 2000).

John Bennett (2001) notes that trainers are leaders of learning and that the servant leader model can inspire an individual to become an exceptional trainer. He goes further in sharing how to become a servant leader by emphasizing getting to truly know our participants, being willing to experiment, finding appropriate ways to acknowledge success, encouraging growth, and seeking feedback for personal growth. The capacity for servant leadership is often gauged by the questions, "do those who are served grow as persons; do they, while being served, become healthier, wiser, freer, more autonomous; more likely themselves to become servants?" (Greenleaf, 1977). The characteristics of servant leadership, though varied depending on the source, are summarized by Spears (2010) as the following qualities:

Listening: Listening receptively and attentively to what is being said
Empathy: Demonstration of acceptance and understanding of others
Healing: Providing healing for self and others to achieve wholeness
Awareness: Understanding the situation and one's own limitations in a holistic way
Persuasion: Seeking to convince others through persuasion and consensus
Conceptualization: Broad-based thinking and visionary concepts
Foresight: Understanding the lessons from the past, reality of the present, and possibilities for the future
Stewardship: Holding the institution in trust for the greater good of society
Commitment to Growth: Interest in personal and professional growth for self and other
Building Community: Building a sense of community among groups and in society

According to Parker & Carroll (2009), leadership development through coaching is an intentional process that facilitates reflective learning, develops the capability to work in collaboration, and creates a culture of integration through shared meaning. They studied the qualities of peer partnering among a group of 22 high-potential leaders in a leadership development course. It was revealed that leadership development draws from the capacities of structural (social and network) ties, relational (interactions and relationships) and cognitive (shared representation and collective meanings).

They elaborated that peer coaching may have a benefit over subordinate coaching by eliminating power dynamics and creating mutual support through comparable levels of experience. The study also found that sponsorship of someone as a coach provides purpose, joy, and leadership development for the sponsor. The servant leader will derive a sense of fulfillment from mentoring, coaching, and growing collaboratively with others (McGee & Trammell, 2001). They concluded that peer dialogue facilitates awareness of self, others, and the environment, serving the leadership and career ends of the individuals concerned.

Stephen Griffith (2007), evaluated transactional, transformational, and servant leadership through a lens of ethics questioning whether the leadership itself was ethical. The basis of ethicality was determined by the lack of coercion, multidirectional influence, and mutuality of purpose. It was postulated that these three leadership styles were subsequent plateaus toward ethical leadership with transactional as the first plateau, followed by transformational, and finally servant. Based on the balance of power within servant leadership and subjugated needs of the leader to that of the follower, a true multidirectional influence occurred. The collaborative nature of the environment strengthens not only the multi-directional influence, but also the mutuality of purpose. Servant leadership thus was positioned as the "ultimate level of ethicality".

Fukuda (2017) stated that effective coaching builds relationships that lead to trust, and through positivity we produce receptiveness. He elaborated on the essentials of effective coaching: patience on the part of both participants, trust by developing a real relationship, listening, positivity, and being a consistent presence. A solid relationship can be created by listening to show you care, positive and supportive communication, as well as a consistent presence. Servant leadership and effective coaching share some of the same qualities aimed to enhance the interactions and relationships of individuals, including listening, empathy, awareness, commitment to growth, and community building. Defining the attributes of these characteristics may show a deeper relationship between coaching and servant leadership.

Difference Between Coaching

There are differences in coaching, formal and informal. Formal coaching involves scheduled meetings with a clear beginning and end, and conversations in "coaching mode", while informal coaching occurs during everyday conversations at work. In coaching, there is a distinction between skills, performance, and developmental coaching. Skills coaching focuses on developing a specific skill, performance coaching is about improving performance over a specific time period, and developmental coaching focuses on issues of personal and professional development or working effectively as a team member. Coaching programs should be grounded in evidence-based research and theory.

They must also be internally branded and championed by the organization, use attraction versus coercion, and allow the freedom to evaluate and evolve the process. The power in coaching comes from strength of participants' questions. Forbes Coaches Council (2018) shared that a powerful question allows someone to engage in the possibility of overcoming whatever obstacle is stopping them from reaching their goals. The goal of a coach is not to give answers to the situations faced by the individual or organization, but to guide them toward their own solutions and hold them accountable to act. The power is in asking the right questions to help the individual or organization discover the right solution, learn powerful lessons about themselves, and grow through the process.

Jim Goodnight (2019) shared the success of a coaching practice at Forge Company in which every employee was assigned a coach, set a personal development plan, and had weekly thirty-minute sessions with their coach. The sessions spent ten minutes each on three general areas of the employee's life: personal, professional, and goals. After six months they saw a rise in employee engagement. Su (2014) postulated that effective coaching should ask questions that emphasize self-reflection and allow the individual to see their own actions from a different perspective or envision a new solution to an old problem. Coaching is a common practice to develop the skills, performance, and development of an individual with the guiding principles of active listening, understanding, and self-discovery to strive for personal and professional growth Finally, Shanta Harper (2012) studied the value of leadership coaching to achieve business value and concluded that it is possible to calculate, using an ROI (return on investment) measure, the value of leadership coaching. However, for an organization to achieve the most value, it must add the components of establishing business objectives around coaching and tie coaching to the objectives with clear communication.

CHAPTER 12

Servant Leadership in The Boardroom

"Gentlemen, you will permit me to put on my spectacles,
for I have not only grown gray but almost blind in the service of my country."
–George Washington, March 15, 1783.

Boards transform leadership through policy governance. Building strong boards have has never been more important. According to Bowen (2008), directors and trustees need to enjoy coming to meetings, and enjoyment is often the product of stimulation and active exchanges with bright colleagues. However, that is not always the case in most boardrooms. Most boards do not seem to understand their mandate; others find their mandate quite complicated than they thought, some are not well-structured, and those with government appointees faces suspicion and risk factors, real or imagined. Worse still, some boards have relationship challenges between the CEOS or directors and the board chair. Ethics is attributed to some of the relationship challenges. Ego is one of them, and directional disagreements are the other factors. If these challenges are resolved and both work together, major efficient and ethical decisions would be made for the benefit of all stakeholders.

Why Have Boards? There are many reasons for having boards. (a) Required by law, (b) Expected by constituents, (c) To provide governance. **What Is Governance then?** *Governance is the coming together of a* **group** *of elected or appointed individuals to* **act as one** *for the purpose of* **guiding** *the organization of which they hold* **trusteeship** *toward the accomplishment of its* **ends** *while establishing appropriate* **boundaries** *for accountability.* The secret of governance lies in **policymaking,** but policymaking of a finely crafted sort. It is not about the board controlling more or less but controlling the **right things** in the **right way.**

There are different types of boards: Ceremonial, Single person Driven, Committee Driven, Management Review, Complaint Driven, Meddling, Rubber-stamping, Advisory, Cheerleader, and Policy Governance.

The Objective of Boards: To create an organizational environment that will increase the likelihood of the **right** people doing the **right** things in the **right** way at the **right** time for the **right** reasons so that the **right** results will be achieved for the **organization.**

What Are the Benefits of Boards? There are many benefits of boards. Some are: More time spent working on important issues, protection from trivia, more staff empowerment, without being staff-driven, greater personal fulfillment for the board, a more secure environment for both the board and administrator, better use of time and resources for both the board and administrator, clarification of roles and responsibilities, and an increased likelihood that the desired results will be reached for the nation/organization.

The question that arises is, if boards are necessary for healthy organizations or nations, why are they inefficient or not achieving the desired results? The answer to this question lies in the problems many boards face. Few are listed below:

- "The only thing boards have in common is that they don't work." (Peter Drucker).
- "What most boards do most of the time is a waste of time." (John Carver).
- "No matter how dedicated or intelligent, people cannot be all they can be in a poor system." (John Carver).

Having noticed how most boards don't work or are dysfunctional; wastes time and operates in a poor system, let's try to find some solutions.

The Solution: The <u>Policy Governance</u> model of board leadership is universally applicable to **ANY** governing board of **ANY** type of organization in **ANY** culture at **ANY** stage of development. It is <u>values-based</u>, conceptually coherent and comprehensive. It is not merely an organizational model, but an <u>integrated</u> system of concepts, process and philosophy.

Four Foundational Pillars of Boards.

Accountability: The board must hold the CEOs or Presidents strictly accountable for policies it has stated. The board cannot hold the CEOs or Presidents accountable for policies it has not stated, nor can it take on itself responsibilities that belong to the CEOs or Presidents.

Empowerment: The board must empower CEOs or Presidents to carry out their responsibilities in an environment reasonably free from fear or uncertainty. The board must draw clear limits on the acceptable activities of CEOs or Presidents.

Servant-leadership: The board must provide strong visionary leadership. The board must be a servant to the owners, for whom it holds the organization in trust.

Clarity of Group Values: A healthy board should have rigorous diversity and members have freedom to express divergent opinions. The board only has authority when it is functioning and speaking as a group; individual members have no independent authority at all. **The board must speak clearly with one voice.** A board member is supposed to become a trustworthy trustee.

Ten Principles of Boards Policy Governance.

1. Board members are trustees for the ownership.
2. The board must speak with one voice or not at all.
3. Board decisions should predominantly be stated in the form of policies.
4. Boards should formulate policies from the "Outside-In."
5. A board Should define and delegate–Not react and ratify.
6. The highest calling of a board using policy governance is to determine the organization's ends.
7. The board should control how the staff operates (Staff Means) only through pre-defined limits.
8. The board must be responsible for designing its own products and processes.
9. The board must forge a relationship with the administrator that provides necessary control with maximum empowerment.
10. Performance must be rigorously monitored, but only against predefined written policy.

Adapted from Carver Guide #1, Basic Principles of Policy Governance, by John Carver 1996.

Ultimately, boards need one ethical voice to achieve the ten principles above. Board members should be able to say what they really mean boldly and fearlessly at board meetings, not at the parking lots.

Comparison of the Four Policy Types.

Ends: What difference will we make? Stated positively, Looks outward. Responsibility – Administrator (CEO or President).

Executive Limitations: What is not allowed? Stated negatively, Looks inward. Responsibility: Administrator (CEO or President).

Board-Staff Linkage: How should board & staff interact? Stated positively, Looks inward. Responsibility: Board Chair.

Governance Process: How should the board operate? Stated positively, Looks inward. Responsibility: Board Chair.

Turning Negatives into Positives: Administrator (CEO/President) feels empowered within these areas.

    a.   Stop until we say go! Activities Approved by the board.

    b.   Go until we say stop! Activities "limited" by the board.

Accountability Vs. Empowerment.

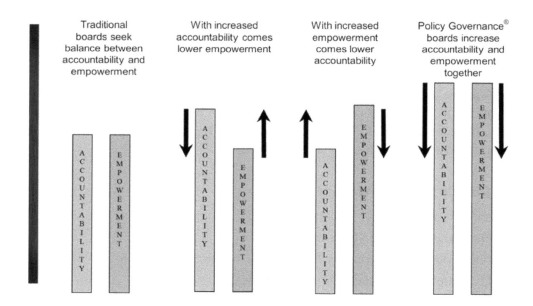

The Products of the Board:

The purpose of the board job is to assure (on behalf of ownership) that the organization achieves what it should and avoids what is unacceptable. While–**L**inking with the ownership, ***assuring*** acceptable administrator performance, **W**riting well-crafted governing policies.

Examples of Monitoring.

- Internal administrative reports
- External reports (i.e., audit/accreditation)
- Direct inspection by the board

Good policy governance is NOT about Budget lines, Personnel practices, Intricacies of programs or curriculum, or Group insurance purchases. It is about values, strategic leadership, vision and reaching the ends. In conclusion, policy governance is a model of leadership that clarifies the roles of board and administration in such a way that both may experience the mutual joy of a fulfilled vision.

CHAPTER 13
Servant Leadership and Ethics

Legality (the law) is the lowest permissible standard of behavior in society.
The highest are moral and ethical values."
– Fred Edwords.

Ethics is simply the moral principles or values that defines what is right or wrong for a person, group, or society. It is the Dos and Don'ts. Ethics is similar to breathing and blinking, with a slight twist. According to Pew Study, we breathe and blink subconsciously, unaware that the average adult on a daily basis takes 18,000 breaths and 15,000 blinks. Similarly, we are unaware that every decision made during a day has ethical ramifications. The reason is simple: All decisions are initiated by motives and results in consequences: were our motives and intentions good or bad, and were the consequences or outcomes good or bad? However, unlike breathing and blinking, which are automatic, humans possess free will and can choose to behave ethically or unethically in a particular situation.

Even if the decision-maker believes he/she is being ethical, someone harmed by the action may think otherwise. Let's look at practical situations. Should you arrive at work early, on time or late? Should you submit adequate work that meets a deadline or submit the highest-quality work possible and miss the deadline? Should you inform your boss about your colleague's questionable work habits? Should the organization incur additional costs for environmental protection technologies not required by law? Should you leave work at the designated time or cancel after-work plans and stay late to finish a project? What about abuse of company resources, lying to employees, email or internet abuse, improper hiring practices, falsifying time or expenses, conflict of interest, discrimination, employee benefits violations or employee privacy breach?

In leadership, ethical behaviors are demonstrated by leaders, who must hold themselves to a higher ethical standard. That is, the code of moral principles and values that govern the behaviors of right or wrong should be exhibited in practicality, advocated and visible. The challenge is contested concepts of ethics, that is, divergent views of what is right or wrong. We all agree that lying is unethical. However, the contested issues are what constitute lying? The answer is in legal standards (Laws or policies), ethical standards (social standard) and personal standard (sphere of free choice). Obviously, there are many ethical gaps in every sphere of human endeavor – greed, deceit, irresponsibility, and lack of moral conscience abounds. According to Yulk et al. (2013), the ethical leader displays an +interrelated characteristic of honesty and integrity, communicates and enforces ethical standards though exhibited behavior, is fair in decisions and distribution of rewards, and shows kindness, compassion, and concern for needs and feelings of others.

Managing ethics entails a couple of actions: *Code of ethics* – a formal statement of the company's values regarding ethics and social issues, *Ethical structures* – systems, positions, and programs like ethics training, *Whistle-blowing* – employee disclosure of illegal, immoral, or illegitimate practices (Williams, 2019).

There are established research frameworks for ethical decision making. These are:

> ***Utilitarian approach*** – moral behavior produces the greatest good for the greatest number.
> ***Individualism approach*** – acts are moral if they promote the individual's long-term interest,
> ***Moral-rights approach*** – humans have fundamental rights and liberties that cannot be taken away by
an individual's decision,
> ***Justice approach*** – moral decisions must be based on standards of equity, fairness, and impartiality.

Talking about justice, there are three types: Distributive justice, Procedural justice, and Compensatory justice. The practicality of ethics is in standards of self, group, society, and a country.

The Ethic of Sustainability.

Whereas corporate social responsibility is to give back to society, the ethics of sustainability is the economic development that generates wealth and meets the needs of current generation while preserving the environment for the needs of future generations (Carroll, 1979). This is demonstrated in the pyramid below:

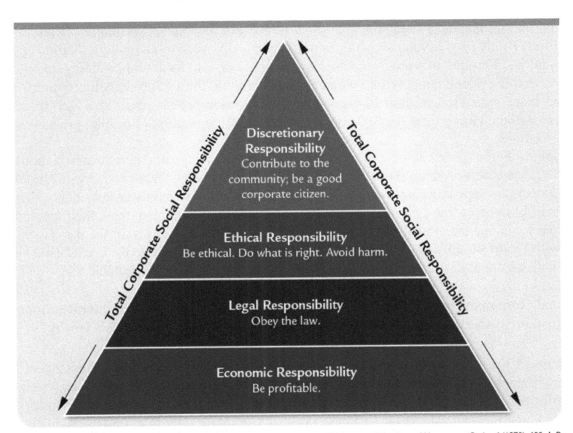

SOURCES: Based on Archie B. Carroll, "A Three-Dimensional Conceptual Model of Corporate Performance," *Academy of Management Review* 4 (1979): 499; A. B. Carroll, "The Pyramid of Corporate Social Responsibility: Toward the Moral Management of Corporate Stakeholders," *Business Horizons* 34 (July–August 1991): 42; and Mark S. Schwartz and Archie B. Carroll, "Corporate Social Responsibility: A Three-Domain Approach," *Business Ethics Quarterly* 13, no. 4 (2003): 503–530.

According to (Carroll, 1979) there are three main responsibilities of organizations. Economic Responsibility: A company's social responsibility to make a profit by producing a valued product or service. Legal Responsibility: A company's social responsibility to obey society's laws and regulations. Ethical Responsibility: A company's social responsibility not to violate accepted principles of right and wrong when conducting its business. Discretionary Responsibilities: The social roles that a company fulfils beyond its economic, legal, and ethical responsibilities. Social Responsiveness: A company's strategy to respond to stakeholders' economic, legal, ethical, or discretionary expectations of social responsibilities. Reactive Strategy: A social responsiveness strategy in which a company does less than what society expects. Defensive Strategy: Company admits responsibility for a problem but does the least required to meet social expectation. Accommodative Strategy: Social responsiveness strategy where a company accepts responsibility for a problem and does all that society expects to solve the problem. Proactive Strategy: Company anticipates a problem before it occurs and does more than society expect to take responsibility for and address the problem.

Practicality of These Ethical Concepts. Sampled Organizations That Practice Them.

In each situation below, an organization/company is listed, and we explain why they meet the definitional criterion. Practical examples are given.

- **Discretionary Responsibilities: This company fulfills beyond its economic, legal, and ethical responsibilities, and this is why?**

Kohls is an example of a company that goes above and beyond its economic, legal, and ethical responsibilities. Kohls runs a volunteer program for their employees to encourage them to give back to their communities. Through this program, employees volunteer with local non-profit organizations. Every organization that five Kohls employees volunteer for, is eligible for a $500 donation. Since 2001, Kohls has donated more than $166 million in corporate grants to non-profits across the U.S. In 2019, Kohls employees contributed more than 300,000 volunteer hours and more than $11 million grants were given to 4,500 organizations.

According to Forbes, one example of a company that has exceptional discretionary responsibilities is Lego. In 2017, there was an analysis on the ethicality of different businesses and organizations (Strauss, 2017). Lego operates their business transparently, and they have no scandals or lawsuits against them. In the analysis of businesses, the Lego brand conducts business fairly and also treats their employees fairly. Not only does Lego operate ethically, they also have supported worthy causes. In the past years, they have partnered with World Wildlife Fund, and they donated portions of their sales to the conservation of wildlife. Operating with excellent discretionary responsibility makes the company respectable.

- **Social Responsiveness: This company's strategy responds to stakeholders' economic, legal, ethical, or discretionary expectations of social responsibilities. And this is why?**

Levi Strauss & Co. is an example of a company that has great social responsiveness. The company has started an initiative to use less water in the production of jeans and to educate consumers on how to expand the life cycle of jeans, while using less water. This initiative aims to create less waste from the garment industry. They have also developed a partnership with Evrnu to create a pair of jeans made only from post-consumer cotton waste. These new jeans allow materials to be efficiently recycled. This partnership is allowing them to sustainably use resources, benefiting all of their stakeholders.

Within the supermarket industry, LifeSource Natural Foods is another example of a company that adheres to social responsiveness. LifeSource is an organic grocery store that has a high emphasis on organic foods, fair labor practices, and sustainability. The company was voted one of the 100 Best Green Companies to Work for in Oregon in 2014 (Kinhal, 2019) and focuses heavily on protecting the environment. By upholding high ethical and moral standards for protecting the environment, LifeSource Natural Foods upholds social responsibilities in abiding by legal obligations and upholding stakeholders' expectations for the company.

Aflac is another company on high social responsibility in ethics. Aflac responds to the community. In the past, they have raised funds to fight pediatric cancer, bone cancer, and blood diseases. Aflac has been on the Ethisphere Institute's World's Most Ethical Companies list for ten years in a row, and it is based on three areas: internal ethical business standards, enabling managers and employees to make good choices and shaping future industry standards. Aflac has proven to take social responsibilities seriously and implement ethical standards throughout the company.

- **Reactive Strategy: This company does less than what society expects. And this is why?**

Monsanto is an example of a company with a reactive strategy that does less than what society expects. Monsanto is responsible for creating a variety of highly toxic and carcinogenic chemicals such as DDT, Agent Orange, and Roundup. These chemicals have caused harm to humans, animals, and the planet. Monsanto is often criticized for its creation and production of Genetically Modified Organisms, or GMOs. Despite large push back from society and stakeholders, Monsanto continues to produce and push for the use of their harmful products because of the profit that they produce.

Equifax is another company that demonstrated reactive strategy by reacting to an issue once the issue had already occurred. On July 29, 2017, Equifax announced that the company had experienced a data breach that affected over 100 million customers' personal information (St. John, 2017). After extensive research and an investigation by a security researcher for the company, it was determined that Equifax was notified about a potential risk of a confidentiality breach but failed to take protective measures to prevent against the possible data breach. Rather than heeding the warnings, Equifax reacted to a situation rather than anticipating the risk ahead of time. Because of the breach, Equifax credibility was lessoned and experienced loss of customers.

- **Defensive Strategy: This company admits responsibility for a problem but does the least required to meet social expectation. And this is why?**

Foxconn is an example of a company with a defensive strategy that admits a problem but does the least required to meet social expectations. Within the last 10 years the company experienced multiple suicide attempts by its employees. These attempts were driven by poor working and living conditions at a company compound in China. In response to the suicide attempts the company installed safety nets rather than attempt to fix the conditions which drove the employees to believe that suicide was their best option. This minimal response to a serious issue illustrates the company's defensive strategy.

Another company that uses a defensive strategy is Justice for Girls. In 2017, a class action settlement agreement was issued against the Ascena Retail Group about the advertising product discounts that was misleading and deceptive and in violation of state consumer protection statutes. The company was made to issue checks or vouchers to over 18.6 million customers. Justice complied on the settlement and customers were given vouchers. The marketing has been better, but there was no apology or public statement issued. This company demonstrates the minimal amount of effort in meeting social expectations of the customers.

- **Accommodative Strategy: This company accepts responsibility for a problem and does all that society expects to solve the problem. And this is why?**

Perdue Foods is an example of a company with an accommodative strategy. They were forced to recall 495 pounds of premade, frozen chicken due to undeclared allergens. The package that the product was sold in stated that the breaded chicken was gluten-free. However, the product contained wheat, an allergen. This confusion occurred due to a mix up when packaging the frozen chicken. In accordance with FDA guidelines, the company was expected by society to recall the product to maintain public safely and they did that swiftly.

American Airlines is another example. This organization focus on customer satisfaction. When flights experience cancelations and complications, customers can often be annoyed or disgruntled by the situation. In most cases, if a customer wishes to receive a type of service recovery, that customer is required to go through a complicated and extensive process of filing paperwork or dealing with customer service. Recognizing that customers experience frustration with service recovery, American Airlines has allowed employees the ability to issue customer complimentary miles whenever needed (Morgan, 2018). This accommodation was not required, but American Airlines established the program in order to better their customers' experiences; understanding that flight cancelations and complications cannot always be avoided.

Another organization using accommodative strategy is Uber. Uber is a company that provides ride shares. Uber has had many issues, especially in inner cities, with the safety of the customers. There are many instances where customers have been killed, abducted, or assaulted by Uber drivers. The company has recognized that the safety of the customers is sometimes compromised, and they have put in place new safety measures and background checks in order to satisfy people who were boycotting Uber for safety reasons. Some of the safety measures that they have implemented are making sure customers have easy access to authorities and background checks on their drivers. This has increased safety; met some expectations and a sign of learning and listening.

- **Proactive Strategy: This company anticipates a problem before it occurs and does more than society expect to take responsibility for and address the problem. And this is why.**

The Toro company is an example of a company with a proactive strategy. A proactive strategy maintains the quality reputation of the company, builds customer goodwill, and increases trust in the company. The Toro company produces commercial riding mowers. In response to finding out that units had defects, they voluntarily recalled 62,000 mowers. They took a proactive response and worked closely with dealers, distributors, and customers throughout the recall to repair and replace the damaged mowers. This proactive response allowed them to keep quality customers, strengthening the business for the future.

Dell is another company that is using a proactive strategy when incorporating sustainable operation strategies. In 2015, Dell was able to adjust their packaging and delivery tactics in order to eliminate over 30 million pounds of packaging that would have been wasted (Lorek, 2015). Dell's headquarters have also been converted so that they run on 100 percent renewable energy while also trying to make their computers 25 percent more energy efficient (Lorek, 2015). Dell already follows environmental codes and rules for their operations and computers while also embracing climate change and the impact the organization can have on protecting the environment.

Finally, Google is another proactive strategy organization working towards a greener future. Google has a comprehensive plan in place. On their website, it discusses how they are developing environmentally friendly services to improve people's lives. They work to inform people on different environmental issues and promote clean and renewable energy. All of these efforts are a part of Google's proactive strategy. They use their resources and put millions of dollars into researching new technology and ways of preventing environmental destruction.

In conclusion, we are all stakeholders in ethics. That means we must all have interest in the well-being of our organization. A stakeholder is someone with interest in organization. Internal stakeholders include employees, leaders, and owners. External stakeholders include suppliers, society, government, creditors, shareholders, and customers. So, how can leader build an ethical organization? Trevino, Hartman, and Brown (2000) proposed the following: Ethical Leadership, Code of Ethics, Ethics Committee, Chief Ethics Officer, Ethics Hotline, Ethics Training and Support for Whistle-blowers.

CHAPTER 14
Servant Leadership and Change

"The world will not change until we do." Jim Williams, The Soul of Politics. A political and Prophetic vision of change, 3, 1994.

Change is imminent, yet difficult to execute. In thinking about change, think about these cultural constructs first: policies, procedures, mindset, values, rituals, religious beliefs, laws (written and unwritten), ideas, customs, beliefs, ceremonies, social institutions, myths and legends, individual identity, arts and behaviors. What progressive effort can change these individual, but related concepts? Then, think about individuals belonging to different cultures, inter alia, national, religion, ethnic group, different generation, social class and workplace or corporate culture. Even the way we debate change have contentious issues. According to Dunoon (2008) contentious issues consist of: (a) No technical or correct answers to be found, (b) multiple interpretations of the problem cannot be resolved simply by the application of facts, evidence and specialist analysis, (c) need to deal with contention and threat: multiple stakeholders working from diverse assumptions, using language differently, (d) takes time to clarify to merge against short-term pressures to achieve results, and (e) have an explicit side (more tangible aspect of the problem) and an implicit side (relatively hidden or subtle aspects of the problem).

Dunoon further proposed a framework for intervening with contentious issues to help build shared understanding as a basis for action. This is in an acronym – ARIES: Attending, Reflecting, Inquiring, Expressing and Synthesizing. **Attending** comprises putting the quality of our attention prior to task achievement in that moment. It is also about identifying what is observable regarding the problem as distinct from what may be inferred. **Reflecting** involves interpreting what is perceived, including drawing on evidence to frame possible interpretations. Reflecting is also about making sense of what is perceived and identifying possible underlying assumptions,

interests, feelings, and knowledge of stakeholders to understand the problem at hand. **Inquiring** comprises of using questioning processes and rationality to build shared meaning as well as identifying powerful questions for stakeholders to aid understanding of the problem. **Expressing** involves declaring own views and rationality in ways that enables others to see more of what matters to you and finding ways to express your deeper thoughts and feelings while maintaining safety. **Synthesizing** encompasses naming an integrated understanding that can be tested with others of the challenges to be faced (the transformational challenge). It is also about identifying one or more relational challenges to the mission, vision or problem faced in a spur of a moment. The hard truth is that if organizations cannot innovate around these challenges and innovate, they die. However, change is difficult because most people resist it for many reasons such as uncertainty, self-interest, lack of understanding, lack of trust, unclear expectations, poor communication or different assessments and goals. Basically, what you don't know could also be intimidating. As an example, I had an updated version of my cell phone and loved the new one. However, uploading the old videos, pictures, and information unto the new one costs me over 45 minutes of uploading, yet I lost some of my videos and pictures in the process. In the end, I wished I had kept my old phone even though the new one was better with more modern features.

There are as many different approaches as possible to guiding an organization through changes. In subsequent chapters, I will summarize few change theories that are practically applicable in leadership Leon de Caluwé and Hans Vermaak (2003) developed a color-coded approach to change. Their approach represents different belief systems and convictions, coded into colors, on how change works; the kind of interventions that might be effective, and how to actually engender cooperation in instituting new approaches (2003). The theory is exhibited in the color-table below:

De Caluwé's Color-Coded Summary

Leon de Caluwé and Hans Vermaak posit that dialogues in organizations based on a multi-paradigm perspective (such as the colors) enhance organizational vitality. The difficulty for change is not in the development of new ideas, but in escaping the old ideas, that determine our thinking. Change is a collective effort and, more often than not, involves people with multiple perspectives on organizational life and multiple definitions of reality. For difficult issues, it is best to involve people from various backgrounds and viewpoints based on collectively considering multiple realities and corresponding paradoxes. Such is the reason for this primmer on organizational change innovation. This author posits that there is a continuum from a yellow-print approach, where the leadership has experience and established credibility with the followers that allows for a more give and take approach, to the other end of the spectrum where the leadership is not well established or where a slow, follower-led change approach such as a white-print approach has more chance for success. Once the leadership team assess where the team and the followers lie on that spectrum, then any number of different approaches to change can be used to successfully guide an organization through a change cycle.

Yellow-Print Thinking

Yellow-print thinking comes from symbols of power like the sun and fire. Yellow-print thinking comes from the socio-political concept about organizations in which the perceived best leadership approach is based on power plays in which followers will only change if their interests are considered.

Blue-Print Thinking

Blue-print thinking is based upon rational design and clear organization. It is similar to the architectural blueprints designed to facilitate effective construction of new buildings. Project management is one of its strongest tools. It is assumed that people or things will change if a clearly specified result is laid down beforehand. Controlling the change by managing, planning, and monitoring the progress is considered feasible. The process and results are almost deemed independent of people. Both outcomes and processes are planned down to the last detail. Change is deemed a rational process aimed at the best possible solution.

Red-Print Thinking

Red-print thinking is used to strategically focus on the emotions of the workers to stimulate them to action; human blood is red. Change equates with people changing their behavior. Leaders seek ways to stimulate people appealing to them to adjust their behavior. Carefulness, steadfastness, and loyalty are relevant attributes for the change agent. The foremost consideration of the red-print change agent is that the human factor plays a vital role. Change agents are good at motivating people.

Green-Print Thinking

Green-print thinking is allowing and supporting people to take ownership of their learning; gives followers the green light. Tapping into the abilities and talents of the followers and providing avenues for them to continue to learn and grow provides a learning stream for the organization. Learning Organizations, as advocated by Senge and Argyris and Schein are examples of this change theory applied in business. Changing and learning are closely linked. People are motivated to discover the limits of their competencies and to involve themselves in the learning situation. The aim is to strengthen the learning abilities of the individual and the learning within the organization. Green-print thinking is concerned with allowing and supporting people to take ownership of their learning. Typical interventions include coaching, simulations, survey feedback, opens-systems planning, action learning, and leadership training. Empathy, creativity, and openness are important attributes of the change agent.

White-Print Thinking

Self-organization is the key concept; white denotes openness, a blank slate. People interact according to their own norms without a map, what to do, or how to get there. New structures and behavior patterns emerge through developmental, learning, and evolutionary processes. The system finds its own optimal dynamic balance. Everything changes autonomously of its own accord. Change agents call on people's strengths, self-confidence, inspiration, and energy.

Edgar Schein Cultural Change Theory

Looking through a yellow-print lens, Edgar Schein (2004) advocated for considering the organizational culture when attempting to understand how to move employees to embrace change. In order to understand the interests of employees, one must learn about the cultural climate of the organization. According to Schein, "the most intriguing aspect of culture as a concept is that it points to phenomena that are below the surface, that are unconscious. In that sense, culture is to a group what personality or character is to an individual" (2004, p.8). Schein defines culture as "a pattern of shared basic assumptions that was learned by a group as it solved its problems of external adaptation and internal integration, that has worked well enough to be considered valid and, therefore, to be taught to new members as the correct way to perceive, think, and feel in relation to those problems" (2004, p. 17).

According to Schein (2004), culture can be analyzed at different levels. The levels range from overt manifestations that one can see, to deeply embedded assumptions. In between these levels are espoused beliefs, values, norms, and rules of behavior (2004). Schein posits that "values are open to discussion, but basic assumptions are so taken for granted that someone who does not hold them is viewed as a foreigner ... and is automatically dismissed (2004, p. 25). Schein's levels of culture could be diagramed as follows:

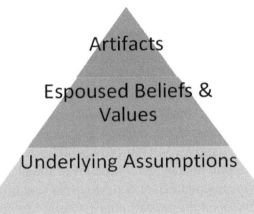

For most observers the easiest way to analyze the culture is at the surface level with the **artifacts**. These include the visible products of the group: language, technology, style, clothing, manners of address, emotional displays, myths and stories about the organization, rituals and so forth (2004, p 26). Unfortunately, artifacts do not provide a reliable source for understanding the culture. It is easy to observe but difficult to decipher. Schein offers an illustration that might help us to better understand why interpreting artifacts can lead to a poor analysis of the culture.

> For example, when one sees a very informal, loose organization, one may interpret that as inefficient if one's own background assumes that informality means playing around and not working. Or alternatively, if one sees very formal organization, one may interpret that to be a sign of lack of innovative capacity, if one's own experience assumes that formality means bureaucracy and formalization, (2004, p 27).

All groups reflect someone's **espoused beliefs and values** which might reflect the original beliefs for the inception of the group or might represent evolved beliefs and values. Group members who influence the group's beliefs and values are the real leaders. When the majority of the group accepts certain values due to a shared social experience, the values become ingrained. Schein offers an illustration: if a leader notes that business will increase if more money is spent on advertisement and increased revenue is the result, then advertisement is aligned with increased revenue. Money spent on advertisement becomes a value to the group (2004, p. 28). A company may state that they value their customers above all else, but reality may be very different. Understanding the group's espoused beliefs and values does help leaders understand and plan for change. To instigate real change innovation, the leaders must understand the culture on a deeper level. The leaders must know and understand the **basic underlying assumptions.** When a "basic assumption comes to be strongly held in a group, members will find behavior based on any other premise inconceivable" (2004, p. 31). This makes change extremely difficult.

Schein notes that "the human mind needs cognitive stability; therefore, any challenge or questioning of a basic assumption will release anxiety and defensiveness" (Schein, 2004, p. 32). Schein describes two "keys to successful culture change: (a) the management of the large amounts of anxiety that accompany any relearning, and (b) the assessment of whether the genetic potential for the new learning is even present" (2004, p. 32). According to Schein "if one does not decipher the pattern of basic assumptions that may be operating, one will not know how to interpret the artifacts correctly or how much credence to give the articulated values" (2004, p 36). Understanding the basic assumptions is a prerequisite to interpreting the artifacts and deciphering the espoused beliefs and values. Culture change is difficult, creates high anxiety in groups, and must be carefully planned and executed. The role of leaders is to investigate the basic underlying assumptions in a culture, build relationships with members of the group so as to better understand those assumptions, and then address the anxiety that change always causes.

Black and Gregersen: Changing Individuals Changes Organizations Theory

Stewart Black and Hal Gregersen, in their book, *Leading Strategic Change (2002),* posit that the best approach to change is to focus on changing individuals first rather than organizations. When a leader chooses to focus on the organization first, they contend that leaders are attacking the problem totally backward. Black and Gregersen contend that change begins with understanding how individuals did the right thing very well. Due to changes in the environment, technology, global, or other issues, eventually the right thing becomes the wrong thing to do. Black and Gregersen provide an example of Motorola in the 1980's which was the industry leader in analog mobile phones. Everyone loved the phones because Motorola was good at producing them. However, the environment shifted, and Motorola was blinded by its current light (success) and opted not to change. Nokia developed digital cell phones while Motorola opted to put more money into developing even better analog phones. Change leaders must understand that people are reluctant to change when they have been successful at doing things one particular way (2002). **"The old right thing becomes the new wrong thing"** (Black and Gregersen, 2002, p.70). **Failure to see** the need for change is the first barrier to effective change.

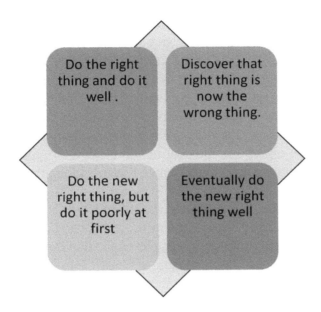

Black and Gregersen contend that people are not blank slates. People contain mental maps of the right thing to do. Leaders must overcome the first barrier to change (brain barrier number one) which is that individuals **fail to see** impending threats and opportunities. Individual workers hold that those mental maps are the correct way to continue because "they are blinded by the light of what they already see – the mental maps that have worked for them in the past" (Black and Gregersen, 2002, p. 43). Part of the difficulty in successfully conducting a change process in an organization is due to the perspective of workers who tend to distort their own importance. Black and Gregersen noted that Barnes and Nobles had a mental map that the best way to sell books was to build more brick-and-mortar buildings. Amazon looked at the market differently and began to sell books online without buildings. Barnes and Noble was blinded by their own light that said more buildings will produce more profitable book sales. They failed to see that the terrain had changed. Leaders must create a sense of urgency if they are to succeed in changing workers mental maps.

In creating a sense of urgency about change leaders begin by combining contrast and confrontation. The leader should seek the best way to provide a high and compelling contrast between the old approach and a new approach. According to Black and Gregersen, the leader should not assume that communicating one time about the changes will suffice (2002). Repeated communication is in order. Portraying the contrast between what has worked in the past and what might work in the future is all important. Creating high contrast, according to Black and Gregersen, involves (a) focusing on the core 20% of what is very different rather than what is slightly different, (b) enhancing (even slightly exaggerating) the simple description between the old and the new, and (c) creating visual images of the old and the new so that the contrast is understood as more than mere words (2008). Black and Gregersen recommend creating high impact confrontation by (a) repeating the message of the old and new maps over and over and over again, (b) focusing on core contrast, and (c) physically ensuring that people cannot easily avoid the experience. Black and Gregersen suggest that you "take time and energy to identify the core 20% that accounts for 80% of the problems rather than the easier approach of working with all the factors of change" (2002, p. 49).

Brain barrier number two is **failure to move**. Black and Gregersen explore why the majority of change projects fail even if a sense of urgency is established and a clear contrast is made. Seeing that the old right thing is now wrong is only half the battle. Employees must also see the new right thing. If the new right thing is not clear, followers will fail to move. Take the example of Xerox. They made large copiers for business, but Canon began making personal small copiers for individuals. At first Xerox failed to admit that the old right thing had become the new wrong thing. "Customers needed document solutions, not just copiers. Customers needed to be grouped by industry need rather than geography (territories) as in the past" (Black and Gregersen, 2002, p. 67). The mental map for many Xerox employees was too difficult to grasp. When it became more than obvious that they needed to shift from the territorial approach they continued to struggle because they could not see a clear path based on the new paradigm. Therefore, Black and Gregersen notes that employees need to not only see the new approach, but they must "**believe** in a new path that will take them from doing the right thing poorly to doing it well" (2002, p 76). Helping them believe involves (a) making sure others see the destination clearly, (b) giving them skills, resources, and tools to reach the destination, and (c) delivering valuable rewards along the journey (Black and Gregersen, 2002).

Brain barrier number three is **failure to finish**. According to Black and Gregersen, failure to finish happens because employees get tired and lost and, therefore, do not go fast enough or far enough. Achieving success requires **champions** in place to reinforce and encourage that the first few times the seeds of change are planted and to applaud the first few steps in their walk of faith. It requires monitoring progress and communicating individual and collective improvement (p. 112). Data is necessary to drive the change process allowing the leaders to know when to champion success and when to adjust the process. Product data must be analyzed on a regular basis. Opinion surveys, focus groups, and individual interviews provide data that allows the leadership to monitor and adjust the change process. Any change initiative should have a limited number of key elements to monitor. Black and Gregersen describe considerations for creating and monitoring the change process: (a) identify key elements to measure, (b) determine a method of measurement, (c) determine the appropriate interval of measurement, (d) develop baseline data, and (e) determine target results (2002). The summary below should assist you in remembering this process.

Brain Barrier # 1 Failure to See	
Blinded by the Light of What We Already See	Old Right Thing Becomes New Wrong Thing

Brain Barrier #2 Failure to Move	
Need Clear Vision or Mental Map of New Destination	Need to Be Willing to Do New Right Thing Poorly at First

Brain Barrier #3 Failure to Finish	
People Get Tired	People Get Lost

Kurt Lewin's Un-freeze, Change and Re-Freeze Theory.

Kurt Lewin introduced the three-step change process in 1951. Hs model is below:

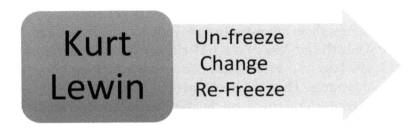

His framework was designed to highlight opposing forces that are often at work when leadership introduces a new change initiative to followers. Lewin, considered by many to be the father of organizational change theories, noted that driving forces are needed to remove restraining forces that are ever-present from employees and often successfully block change initiatives.

Lewin introduced the three-step process to assist leaders in framing their organizational change process that would help them increase driving forces and diminish restraining forces. According to Kritsonis (2007), Lewin posited that these forces must be analyzed and subsequently un-frozen before the leader can begin a change process. The conceptual framework of un-freezing, changing, and re-freezing has served many leaders well as they approach a significant change process. Lewin suggested that the status quo is considered the equilibrium state, and considerable force is necessary to un-freeze the status quo. Un-freezing can be accomplished in three ways: (a) increase the driving force, (b) decrease the restraining forces, and (c) a combination of the two. Robbins (2002) identifies some activities that can assist in the unfreezing step: motivate participants by preparing them for change, build trust and recognition for the need to change, and actively participate in recognizing problems and brainstorming solutions within a group. Lewin espoused that motivation for change must be generated before change can occur.

Lewin's second step in the process of changing behavior is movement. In this step, it is necessary to move the target system to a new level of equilibrium. Three actions that can assist in the movement step include (a) persuading employees to agree that the status quo is not beneficial to them and encouraging them to view the problem from a fresh perspective; (b) working together on a quest for new, relevant information; and (c) connecting the views of the group to well-respected, powerful leaders who also support the change. The third step in Lewin change cycle is re-freezing. Lewin believes that followers would revert to the old way of doing things unless a special effort to emphasize the new approach is employed. The purpose of refreezing is to stabilize the new equilibrium resulting from the change by balancing both the driving and restraining forces. One action that can be used to implement Lewin's third step is to reinforce new patterns and institutionalize them through formal and informal mechanisms including policies and procedures. Failure to make the new change approach part of the new culture is where many change initiatives fail.

John Kotter's Eight-Step Change Process

John Kotter, a world-renowned expert on leadership from the Harvard Business School, has provided an eight-step process that systematicaly takes an organization though the change process. He conveys that simply providing data analysis regarding the need for change is not enough to generate change (Cohen, 2005). Kotter suggests that leaders show followers truth to influence their **feelings**. The process of analysis-think-change is ineffective while the process of **see-feel-change** is powerful. According to Kotter "Highly successful organizations know how to overcome antibodies that reject anything new. They know how to grab opportunities and avoid hazards. They see the bigger leaps are increasingly associated with winning big. They see that continuous gradual improvement, by itself, is no longer enough" (Kotter, 2002, p 2). The eight steps are summarized below.

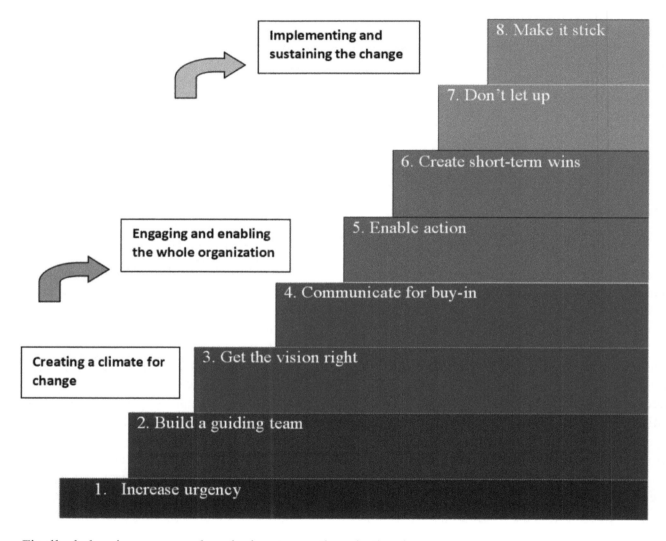

Finally, below is an approach and when to use them in the change process.

1. Establishing a Sense of Urgency

Examining the market and competittive realities	Identifying and discussing crisis, potential crisis, and major oportunties

2. Creating the Guiding Coalition

Putting together a group with enough power to lead change	Getting the group to work together like a team

3. Developing a Vision and Strategy

Creating a vision to help direct the change effort	Creating a strategy for achieving the vision

4. Communicating the Change Vision

Using every vehicle possible to constanting communicate the new vision and strategies	Having the guiding coalistion role model the behavior expected of employees

5. Empowering Broad Based Action

Getting rid of obstacles	Changing systems of structures that undermine the change vision	Encouraging risk taking and nontraditional ideas, activities, and action

6. Generating Short-Term Wins

Planning for visible improvements in performance or "wins"	Creating those wins	Visibly recognizing and rewarding people who madethe wins possible

7. Cosolidating Gains and Producing More Change

Using increased credibility to change all systems, structures, and policies	Hiring, promoting, and developing people who can implement the change vision	Reinvigoring the process with new projects, themes , and chagne agents

8. Achoring New Approaches in the Culture

Creating better performance through better leadership and more effective management	Articulating the connections between new behaviors and organizational success	Developing means to ensre leadership development and succession

CHAPTER 15
Steward Leadership and Servant Leadership

"While God has done His part in creating a world capable of providing what we need, we have not done our part in the stewardship of it, in seeing that it gets to the end of the line, to the poorest and the neediest." – Wess Stafford.

Steward leadership models identified by Robert Clinton (1989), is one of the least developed leadership concepts. We begin with the Classical Steward definition. A steward is one who faithfully and efficiently manages the property or resources belonging to another in order to achieve the owner's objectives. Steward leadership existed as far back as ancient Chinese, Egyptian, Greek, Roman, and Jewish history. Stewards were slaves that were trained from an early age to oversee the rural farm, large households, businesses, financial affairs, and even civic duties. Common words for the steward are *Hebrew 'al habbayit (from 'al, over, and bayit, house), one who oversees the affairs of a household, an important official of the state. Greek oikonomos, from oikos (house, household) and nemo (to distribute, manage), one who manages or administrates a household and its affairs, a state official. Latin- villicus, the farm overseer or steward.*

Stewards were expected to practice management techniques that were a precursor of modern management practice. This includes always learning, trained for management, knows what the master/owner knows, manages resources for maximum efficiency and growth, does not expect subordinates to serve him, demonstrates by example how a job is to be done, and rewards good workers.

Biblical Perspective.

God is affirmed as the ultimate owner of all things (Ps. 24:1, Deut. 8:10-18). People are God's representatives who manage His creation and spiritual resources (Genesis 1:28-30, 1 Peter 4:10). Faithfulness in stewardship will be rewarded with greater responsibilities and resources.

Stewards exhibited a new kind of leadership that serves (modeled by Jesus, Matthew 20:25-28)

The relationship between the owner and steward is critical to effective stewardship. Resources are given to us in varying amounts based on the master's choice and our faithfulness. The primary purpose of stewardship is to grow the resources and manage risk. A steward is most effective if he/she focuses on the rights and goals of the master…not on what he personally wants to accomplish. Masters and stewards experience a reciprocal relationship of mutual understanding and mutual participation in the rewards. Stewards are accountable for their actions and results.

Distinction between Stewardship and Steward Leadership.

Stewardship: *The faithful and efficient management of the property or resources belonging to another in order to achieve the owner's objectives.*

Steward Leadership: *To manage the efficient use and growth of organizational resources, and to lead the staff and activities of the organization as a steward, in order to achieve the mission according to the objectives of the owners and stakeholders.*

The resources we steward are Money, People/employees, Personal gifts, talents, abilities, Time, Products and services, our children, the earth/environment, our bodies, our calling/the organizational mission. Who are the Owners of the Resources We Steward? God (ultimate Owner), Stockholders (publicly traded companies), Business owners (privately held), Stakeholders (implicit owners of nonprofit organizations). Therefore, anyone who is leading a publicly traded company, a nonprofit organization, or is a professional manager in a privately held company, is a steward.

The focus of Steward Leadership:

The lens of ownership: Focuses the steward leader's perspective on the rights and purposes of the owner(s) of the resources. **The lens of motivation**: Focuses the steward leader's altruistic motive that drives self-less behavior for the benefit of others. **The lens of accountability**: Focuses the steward leader on *who* the leader is accountable to and *what* he or she is accountable for.

The Developing Stages of Steward Leadership are: (a) Accountability Stewardship, (b) Sustainability Stewardship, (c) Growth Stewardship, and (d), and Investment Leadership.

Stewardship as accounting: "At the moment you have 40 sheep." No attempt is made at growing the resources but only at giving the owner an accurate count of what he owns at the moment.

Stewardship as sustainability: "Last year you gave me 40 sheep to care for. I have fed them and kept them healthy, so you still have 40 sheep." Sustaining or conserving the resources in perpetuity is the primary goal (custodial care).

Stewardship as growth: "Last year you gave me 40 sheep, and I have increased the herd to 60 sheep." Growing the resources was the responsibility of each of the stewards in the parable of the talents ("put this money to work", Lk. 19:13).

Stewardship as investment: "Last year you gave me 40 sheep, and I have increased the size of the herd to 60 sheep, but I also sold 10 goats that generated a profit you can reinvest in whatever way you desire." In this most mature form of stewardship, generating operational surpluses (i.e., profit) is important in order to have resources that can be reinvested into further ministry or resources.

Difference Between A Servant Leader and a Steward Leader.

	Servant Leadership	Steward Leadership
Core identity	*Servant*	*Steward*
Motivation for leadership	*Altruism (selfless pursuit of the interests of others)*	*Responsibility to the stakeholders, altruism, personal fulfillment*
Characteristics	*Service, selflessness, empowering others*	*The same, plus accountability, faithfulness, knows the master (relationship), mission-focused, non-ownership, and acts with delegated authority*
Primary Action	*Serve people's highest priority needs "Servant first, leader second"*	*Lead the organization to accomplish the desires and objectives of stakeholders. Leverage and grow the resources*
Goal of leadership	*Empowered followers*	*Fulfilled mission Sustainable organization*

As seen from the table above, the steward leadership model addresses: (a) impact of non-ownership on leadership, (b) resource management, (c) relationship with owner, (d) owner/stakeholder accountability, (e) fiduciary accountability. Thus, the basic principles in this type of leadership are clear: Steward leaders recognize that they are not owners, but only trustees of the resources belonging to another; know who they are accountable to and what they are accountable for, maintain close relationships with the owner(s) of the resources in order to know the owner's goals and intentions, and manage resources for maximum efficiency and growth (Rodin, 2010).

Steward leaders ensure that the practical needs of employees are met, develop employees who view themselves as stewards too (under-stewards), live as servants to others, are comfortable with the risks associated with growing and investing resources (Brattgard, 2014). Steward leaders manage a wide range of resources (things, skills, people, money, environment, etc.), lead with delegated authority along with a latitude of freedom in decision-making, expect greater responsibilities and resources as they faithfully carry out their stewardship, and redirect resources when necessary to maximize return-on-investment. Further, they are allowed to maintain a reasonable personal standard of living from the resources, lead out of character, not competence, and experience joy and fulfillment in their work as stewards.

Questions for modern-day steward leader are: How well do you understand your role as a steward leader? What kind of ongoing relationship are you developing with the owner(s) of the resources you manage? (With God? Stockholders? Stakeholders?) At what stage of stewardship are you leading? (Accounting? Sustainability? Growth? Investment?) What would God say to you about how you have managed His resources? How are you helping others to be stewards as well? Peers? Employees? Those you mentor?

CHAPTER 16
Concluding thoughts

Leaders touch a heart before they ask for a hand – John Maxwell.

What is the use of theory if not applicable to daily life or work situation in leadership? It is only through practice that individuals can relate to a theory. Basically, the theory of a fire burn is different from practically touching the naked fire and feeling the sensational buns in your vein to the core that you jump and drop the fire without thinking of where you will land. I believe this book has demonstrated the practicality of this theory in practice.

The practicality was measurable with many conceptual frameworks for assessing servant leadership. Grilled through the test of categories, including integrity, humility, servanthood, caring for others, empowering others, developing others, visioning, goal setting, leading, modeling, team-building, and shared decision making, servant leadership stood the test. In change, ethics, taking care of the environment and stewardship, servant leadership stands tall. The book placed these qualities in a conceptual framework of four categories of orientation: character, people, task and process and development into a self-assessment. The book clarified "people-orientation" as how the leader relates to others and involves developing, empowering, and caring for others. A people-oriented approach is concerned with the social and emotional aspects and involves compassion and interest in developing the potential of others.

We live in an agile world of quick services and open access to technology. The guiding principles of agile leadership include autonomous teams as the basic problem-solving structure and a humanistic approach that values employees. Autonomous, or self-organized teams consist of individuals that support one another, welcome personal learning and feedback, openness, team spirit, and camaraderie (Parker, Holesgrove & Pathak, 2015). In self-organized teams, the interactions build connectivity, honest communication, respect, trust, and alignment to common goals, and these are clear attributes of servant leaders. The supportive, open, collaborative qualities of trust and continued growth are also characteristics of servant leaders.

Now, let's put the entire book to test again, using Robert Greenleaf 's servant leadership measuring tool: "do those who are served grow as persons; do they, while being served, become healthier, wiser, freer, more autonomous; more likely themselves to become servants?" Here is an opportunity to grade yourself as a leader. Are those you are serving growing in wisdom and knowledge? Are they becoming healthier, wiser, freer? Autonomous to do exactly what you have been doing so that they can hold the fort in your absence, and can they serve from the heart with dignity as you? Finally, do you make it easier for them to follow your style and achieve more than you? The final question leads to another question of whether they are "more likely themselves to become servants? There is value in setting an example as a servant leader and modeling the way. Remember to serve first!

References

3M (Minnesota Mining and Manufacturing) Mission and Vision Statement Analysis. Retrieved from: 3M Mission Statement 2021 | 3M Mission & Vision Analysis (mission-statement.com)

Aflac: Leading on Ethics by Example. Mother Nature Network.

Anderson, H. & Foley, E. (1998). *Mighty stories, dangerous rituals: weaving together the human and the divine*. Jossey-Bass Publishers.

Anselm Academics. Uber safety apps. NBC news. https://www.nbcnews.com/tech/innovation/uber-introduces-new-safety-features-including-911-access-its-app-n865161 (Accessed September 19, 2019).

Arbuckle, M. & Konisky, D. (2015). The role of religion in environmental attitudes. *Social Science Quarterly*, 96(5), 1244-1263. https://doi.org/10.1111/ssqu.12213

Argyris, C. (1976). *Increasing leadership effectiveness*. New York: Wiley.

Axelrod, S. D. (2012). "Self-awareness": At the Interface of Executive Development. Academics.

Baker, J. (2016). Native American contributions to a Christian theology of space. *Studies in World Christianity*, 22(3), 234-246. https://doi.org/10.3366/swc.2016.0158

Baldner, G. (2012). Successful Servant Leadership. La Crosse: D. B. Reinhart Institute for Ethics.

Balls-Berry, J, Sinicrope P., Valdez Soto, M., Albertie, M., Major-Elechi B., John, Y., Brockman, T., bock, M., & Patten, C. (2018). Using garden cafes to engage community stakeholders in health research. *PLOS ONE*, 13(8): e0200483. https://doi.org/10.1371/journal.pone.0200483

Bebbington, D. (1989). Evangelicalism in modern Britain: a history from the 1730s to the 1980s. Unwin Hyman.

Belton, L. W. (2018). The intentional servant leader. Greenleaf Center for Servant Leadership.

Belton. L. W. (2018). *The intentional servant leader: Premise and practice*. The Greenleaf Center of Leadership.

Bendaly, L. (2019). Thirty Awesome *Coaching Questions for Leaders*. Retrieved from https://hr-gazette.com/30-awesome-coaching-questions-for-leaders/

Bennett, J.L. (2001). Trainers as Leaders of Learning. *Training and Development*. 55(3) 43-44.

Blanchard, K. (1991). Servant Leadership. Condensed from *The Blanchard Management Report*. Retrieved from www. http://www.appleseeds.org/Blanchard_Serv-Lead.htm

Block, P. (2008). *Community: structure of belonging*. San Francisco, CA: Berrett-Koehler Publishers, Inc.

Block, P. (2018). *Community: The structure of belonging* (2nd ed.). Berrett-Koehler Publishers,

Bookless, D., (2008). Christian mission and environmental issues: an evangelical reflection. *Mission Studies,* 25, 37-52. https://doi:10.1163/157338308X293891

Bowen, W. G. (2008). The board's book: An insider's guide for directors and trustees. W.W Norton & Company.

Boyd, H. (1999). Christianity and the environment in the American public. *Journal for the Scientific Study of Religion,* 38 (1), 36-44.

Bratton, S. (2012). The megachurch in the landscape: adapting to changing sale and managing integrated green space in Texas and Oklahoma, USA. *Worldviews,* 16(1), 30-49. https://doi.org/10.1163/156853511X617795

Bredewold, F., Hermus, M., & Trappenburg, M. (2020). 'Living in the community' the pros and cons: A systematic literature review of the impact of deinstitutionalization on people with intellectual and psychiatric disabilities. Journal of Social Work, 20(1), 83-116. doi:10.1177/1468017318793620

Brooks, D. (2015). *The road to character.* caring leaders. Concepts and Connections: A Newsletter for Leadership Educators, 8(3), 1-5.

Brooks, R. (2020, November 14). All the Things that Google's Company Culture Gets Right. Retrieved from https://peakon.com/us/blog/workplace-culture/google-company-culture/

Bryman, A. (2008). *Social Research Methods* (3rd ed.). Oxford University Press.

Cisco – https://blogs.cisco.com/diversity/acting-on-our-core-values

Coca-Cola (2020) Mission, Vision, & Values: The Coca-Cola Company. Retrieved from Mission, Vision & Values: The Coca-Cola Company (coca-cola.com.sg)

Cogen, P. (2017). Communication skills: Improve your communication skills, build trust, and become successful now. Lexington Press.

Crippen, C. (2005). Servant-leadership as an effective model for educational leadership and

Crippen, C. (2010). Serve, teach, and lead: It's all about relationships. Insight: A Journal of.

Czembrowski, P., Laszkiewicz, E., Kronenberg, J., Engstrom, G., & Andersson, E. (2019). Valuing individual characteristics and the multifunctionality of urban green spaces: the integration of sociotope mapping and hedonic pricing. *PLoS ONE,* 14(3): e0212277. https://doi.org/10.1371/journal.pone.0212277

De Braine, R. & Verrier, D. (2007). Leadership, Character, and Its Development: A Qualitative Exploration. *Journal of Human Resource Management.* 5(1) 1-10. doi: 10.4102/sajhrm. v5i1.102

De Caluwé, L., & Vermaak, H. (2003). *Learning to change: A guide for organizational change agents.* London: Sage Publications.

De Caluwé, L, & Vermaak, H. (2004). Change paradigms: An overview. *Organizational Development Journal, 22*(4) 9-18. http://findarticles.com/p/articles/mi_qa5427/is_200401/ai_n21363013.

Dunoon, D. (2008) *In the leadership mode,* Trafford Publishing.

Ebener, D. R. (2011). Servant leadership and a culture of stewardship. *Priest, 67*(2), 17-21.

Eckberg, D.& Blocker, T. (1989). Varieties of religious involvement and environmental concern: testing the Lynn White thesis. *Journal for the Scientific Study of Religion, 28*(4), 509-17.

Falcone, P. (2016). *The Leader-as-Coach: 10 Questions You Need to Ask to Develop Employees.* Retrieved from https://www.shrm.org/resourcesandtools/hr-topics/organizational-and-employee-development/pages/10-questions-you-need-to-ask-to-develop-employees.aspx

Ferch, S. R. (2012). *Forgiveness and power in the age of atrocity: Servant leadership as a way.*

Forbes Coaches Council. (2018). *16 Powerful Questions Coaches Ask Their Clients to Help Achieve Their Goals.* Retrieved from https://www.forbes.com/sites/forbescoachescouncil/2018/06/21/16-powerful-questions-coaches-ask-their-clients-to-help-achieve-their-goals/#62bea88665e0

Ford–https://corporate.ford.com/about/culture/do-the-right-thing.html

Ford–https://corporate.ford.com/careers/inclusive-hiring/diversity/leading-the-way.html

Fukuda, M. (2017). The 5 Essentials to Effective Coaching. Retrieved from www.entrepreneur.com/article/292877

Gardner, G. (2003). Religion and the quest for a sustainable world. *The Humanist,* 10-15. (Adapted and abridged from chapter eight, "Engaging Religion in the Quest for a Sustainable World," 2003, A Worldwatch Institute Report on Progress Toward a Sustainable Society, 2003, W.W. Norton and Company.

Gentry, W.A., Weber, T.J. & Sadri, G. (2010). *Empathy in the Workplace: A Tool for Effective Leadership.* Retrieved from https://www.ccl.org/wp-content/uploads/2015/04/EmpathyInTheWorkplace.pdf

Gillham, A., Gillham, E., & Hansen, K. (2015). Relationships among coaching success. Paulist Press.

Goodnight, J. (2019). *Interpersonal and Organizational Excellence II: Session 2.* [Lecture].

Google. (n.d.). Ten things we know to be true. Google Philosophy: Retrieved from https://www.google.com/about/philosophy.html

Grant, A.M. & Hartley, M. (2013). Developing the leader as coach: insights, strategies and tips for embedding coaching skills in the workplace. *Coaching: An International Journal of Theory, Research and Practice.* 102-115. doi.org/10.1080/17521882.2013.824015

Grant, T. (2010, June 9). Dr. Sharon K. Stoll on John Wooden. [Video]. YouTube.

Greenleaf, R. (1996). *Seeker and servant: reflections on religious leadership.* Jossey-Bass Publishers.

Greenleaf, R. (2008). *The servant as leader.* Greenleaf Center for Servant Leadership.

Greenleaf, R.K. (1977). *Servant Leadership: A Journey into the Nature of Legitimate Power & Greatness.* Paulist Press.

Greenleaf, R. K. (2002). Servant leadership: A journey into the nature of legitimate power. Greenleaf Center for Servant Leadership.

Greenleaf, R. K. (2008). *The servant as leader.* Robert K. Greenleaf Center.

Greenleaf, R., Fraker, A. and Spears, L. (1996). *Seeker and servant.* Jossey-Bass.

Griffith, S.D. (2007). *Servant Leadership, Ethics and the Domains of Leadership.* Retrieved from https://pdfs.semanticscholar.org/ec83/cac51c724a92e79cb3cc46712f2ee85cf2a6.pdf

Harper, S. (2012). The Leader Coach: A Model of Multi-Style Leadership. *Journal of Practical Consulting.* 4(1). 22-31.

Hayne, P. (2000). The Economic Way of Thinking (9th ed.). Prentice Hall.

Helge, B. (2012). God's stewards: A theological study of the principles and practice of stewardship.

Henry Ford's Anti-Semitism–https://www.pbs.org/wgbh/americanexperience/features/henryford-antisemitism/

Holy Bible. English Standard Version. (2016).

Hubert, J., & Stuart, D. (1980-updated 2001). *A Five-Stage Model in of the Mental Activities Involved in Directed Skill Acquisition.*

Izzo, J. & Vanderwielen, J. (2018). *The purpose revolution: how leaders create engagement and competitive advantage in an age of social good.* Oakland, CA: Berrett-Koehler Publishers.

Jones, L.B. (1995). *Jesus, CEO: Using Ancient Wisdom for Visionary Leadership.* MJF Books.

Keith, K. (2010). *The key practices of servant leadership.*

Keller, D. K. (2006). *The Tao of Statistics: A Path To Understanding With No Math.* Sage Publications.

Kemp, T.J. (2009). Is Coaching an Evolved Form of Leadership? Building a Transdisciplinary Framework for Exploring the Coaching Alliance. *International Coaching Psychology Review.* 4(1) 105-110.

Ken, T. (1709). Doxology. https://www.christianitytoday.com/history/issues/issue-31/where-did-we-get-doxology.html

Kingsley, M. (2019). Climate change, health and green space co-benefits. *Health Promotion and Chronic Disease Prevention in Canada Research, Policy and Practice,* 39(4), 131-135. https://doi.org/10.24095/hpcdp.39.4.04

Kinhal, V. (2019, n.d.). *10 Companies That Are Helping Protect the Environment.* Retrieved September 21, 2019, from lovetoknow: https://greenliving.lovetoknow.com/eco-friendly-products/10-companies-that-are-helping-protect-environment

Koehrsen, J. (2015). Does religion promote environmental sustainability? Exploring the role of religion in local energy transitions. *Social Compass,* 62(3), 296-310. https://doi.org/10.1177/0037768615587808

Kohl's. (2018). *About Kohl's.* Retrieved from https://corporate.kohls.com/company/about-kohl-s

Kohl's. (2018). *Diversity and Inclusion.* Retrieved from https://corporate.kohls.com/company/diversity—-inclusion

Krile, J. F. (2006). *The Community Leadership Handbook: Framing Ideas, Building Relationships and Mobilizing Resources.* Fieldstone Alliance.

Kritsonis, A, (2005), Comparison of Change Theories, *International Journal of Scholarly Academic Intellectual Diversity, 8(1). 1-7.*

Kwik Trip. (2021). *Our Story.* Retrieved from https://www.kwiktrip.com/our-story

Kyte, R. (2012). *An Ethical Life: A Practical Guide to Ethical Reasoning.* Winona, MN: Anselm Academic.

Kyte, R. (2016). *Ethical Business: Cultivating the Good in Organizational Culture.* Anselm Academic.

Lambert, L. (2009). Spirituality Inc.: Religion in the American workplace. New York University Press.

Law, T. (2019, November 10). 15 seriously Inspiring mission and vision STATEMENT EXAMPLES. Retrieved March 29, 2021, from https://www.oberlo.com/blog/inspiring-mission-vision-statement-examples

Leopold, A. (1949). *A Sand County almanac & other writing on ecology and conservation.* (C. Meine, Ed.). New York, NY: The Library of America.

Lewin, K., Lippitt, R., & White, R. K. (1939). Patterns of aggressive behavior in Lewin, Kurt groups, Experiential learning, and action research.

Lorek, L. (2015, October 24). *Going Green is Good for Dell and the Environment.* Retrieved from http://www.siliconhillsnews.com/2015/10/24/going-green-is-good-for-dell-and-the-environment/

Louv, R. (2011). *The nature principle: human restoration and the end of nature-deficit disorder.*

Lutzenhiser, M. & Netusil N. (2001). The effect of open spaces on a home's sale price. *Contemporary Economic Policy*, 19(3), 291-298.

Macias, T. (2015). Risks, trust, and sacrifice: social structural motivators for environmental change. *Social Science Quarterly,* 96 (5), 1264-1276. https://doi.org/10.1111/ssqu.12201

Marschall, M. & Stolle, D. (2004). Race and the city: neighborhood context and the development of generalized trust. *Political Behavior,* 26, 125-153.

Maxwell, N. (2008). From Knowledge to Wisdom: A Revolution for Science and the Humanities.

Mayo Clinic Mission and Values (2021) Retrieved from: Mayo Clinic Value Statements–About Us–Mayo Clinic

McDonalds. (2019). *Our Mission and Values.* Retrieved from McDonalds: https://corporate.mcdonalds.com/corpmcd/our-company/who-we-are/our-values.html

McGee-Cooper, A. & Trammell, D. (2001). *The Essentials of Servant Leadership: Principles in Practice.* Retrieved from http://amca.com/amca/wp-content/uploads/The-Essentials-of-Servant-Leadership.pdf

Meier, D. (2000). *The Accelerated Learning Handbook.* McGraw-Hill Companies, Inc.

Minton, E., Jeffrey Xie H., Gurel-Atay, E., Kahle, L. (2018). Greening up because of God: the relations among religion, sustainable consumption, and subjective well-being. *International Journal of Consumer Studies,* 42, 655-663. https://doi.org/10.1111/ijcs.12449

Mitchell, R. & Popham F. (2008). Effect of exposure to natural environment on health inequalities: an observational population study. *The Lancet,* 372 (9650), 1655-60.

Mitchell, R., Richardson, E., Shortt, N. & Pearce, J. (2015). Neighborhood environments and socioeconomic inequalities in mental well-being. *American Journal of Preventive Medicine,* 49(1), 80-84.

Moore. J. (2019, July 9). *Leadership and contemplation.* Lecture for SVLD 531 at Viterbo University, La Crosse, WI.

Moreno, C. (2015, February 10). *Doing Their Part: 3 Excellent Examples of Corporate Social Responsibility.* Retrieved September 21, 2019, from Autodesk: https://www.autodesk.com/redshift/doing-their-part-3-excellent-examples-of-corporate-social-responsibility/

Morgan, B. (2018, March 14). *10 Companies That Arm Employees with Tools to Fix Customer Problems.* Retrieved September 21, 2019, from Forbes: https://www.forbes.com/sites/blakemorgan/2018/03/14/10-companies-that-arm-employees-with-tools-to-fix-customer-problems/#3a681cac4a30

Msa. "Chick-Fil-A Mission Statement 2021: Chick-Fil-A Mission & Vision Analysis." *Mission Statement Academy*, 11 June 2020, mission-statement.com/chick-fil-a/.

Nakai, P. (2005). The Crucial Role of Coaching in Servant-Leader Development. *The International Journal of Servant-Leadership.* 1(1) 213-228.

Oldenburg, R. (2001). *Celebrating the third place: inspiring stories about the "great good places" at the heart of our communities.* Marlowe & Company.

Our Story. *Hobby Lobby Newsroom.* Retrieved at newsroom.hobbylobby.com/corporate-background/.

Page, D & Wong, T.P. (2000). A Conceptual Framework for Measuring Servant-Leadership. In S. Adjibolooso (Ed.), *The human factor in shaping the course of history and development.* American University Press.

Parker, D.W. & Holesgrove, M. (2015). Improving productivity with self-organized teams and agile leadership. *International Journal of Productivity and Performance Management.* 112-128. doi: 101108/IJPPM-10-2013-0178

Parker, P & Carroll, B. (2009). Leadership Development: Insights from a Careers Perspective. 5(2) 261-283. doi: 10.1177/1742715009102940

Paul, W.K., Smith, C.K. & Dochney, B.J. (2012). Advising as Servant Leadership: Investigating the Relationship. *NACADA Journal. 32*(1). 53-62.

Peach, T. (2019). *Why We Quit: The Real Reasons Why Pastors Leave Ministry Forever.* Psychoanalytic Inquiry, 32(4), 340-357. doi:10.1080/07351690.2011.609364

Pope Francis. (2008). Address to the clergy of the diocese of Bolzano-Bressanone. *AAS* 100, 634.

Pope Francis. (2015). Encyclical letter Laudato si' of the Holy Father Francis on care for our common home. Vatican City, Italy: Vatican Press.

Pope Paul IV. (1971). Apostolic letter octogesima adveniens. *AAS,* 63, 416-417.

Potwarka, L., Kaczynski A., & Flack A. (2008). Places to play association of park space and facilities with healthy weight status among children. *Journal of Community Health,* 33(5) 344-350.

Putnam, R. (2000). *Bowling alone: the collapse and revival of American community.* New York, NY: Simon & Schuster Paperbacks.

Rainer, T.S. (2016). *Who Moved My Pulpit? Leading Change in the Church.* B&H Publishing

Redlawsk, D. (2002). Hot cognition or cool consideration? Testing the effects of motivated reasoning on political decision making. *Journal of Politics,* 64(4), 1021-1044.

Robbins, S. (2003), *Organizational Behavior* (10th ed). Prentice Hall.

Rodin, R. S. (2012). Stewards in the kingdom: A theology of life in all its fullness. IVP Academics.

Rodin, S. K. (2010). The steward leader. IVP Academics.

Rooney, D., McKenna, B. & Liesch, P. (2010). Wisdom and Management in the Knowledge Economy, Routledge.

Roseneau, J. (1980). *The Scientific Study of Foreign Policy* (Rev. Ed.). London. Pp. 19-31.

Saint John Paul II. (1979). Encyclical letter redemptor hominus. *AAS,* 71, 287.

Schein, E. (2004), *Organizational Culture and Leadership* (3rd Ed.). Jossey-Bass, Wiley Inprint.

Severson, A. & Coleman, E. (2015). Moral frames and climate change policy attitudes. *Social Science Quarterly*, 96(5), 1277-1290. https://doi.org/10.1111/ssqu.12159

Shapiro, R. (2004). *The Hebrew prophets: selections annotated and explained.* Woodstock, VT:

Shih-Ying, Y. (2008). A Process View of Wisdom. *Journal of Adult Development*, 1-12

Silberman, M.L & Hansburg, F. (2000). *PeopleSmart: Developing Your Interpersonal Intelligence.* Berrett-Koehler Publishers.

Sipe, J. W., & Frick, D. M. (2015). *Seven pillars of servant leadership: practicing the wisdom of leading by serving.* Mahwah: Paulist.

Spears, L. C. (2000). On character and servant-leadership: Ten characteristics of effective leadership. Robert Greenleaf Center of Servant Leadership.

Spears, L.C. (2010). Character and Servant Leadership: Ten Characteristics of Effective, Caring Leaders. *The Journal of Virtues & Leadership.* 1(1). 25-30.

St. John, A. (2017, September 21). *Equifax Data Breach: What Consumers Need to Know.* Retrieved from https://www.consumerreports.org/privacy/what-consumers-need-to-know-about-the-equifax-data-breach/

Starbucks (2021) Culture and Values. Retrieved from Culture and Values: Starbucks Coffee Company

Sternberg, R. J. (2013). Perspectives: Leadership styles for academic administrators. Lawrence Erlbaum Associates.

Stolle, D., Soroka, S. & Johnston, R. (2008). When does diversity erode trust? Neighborhood diversity, interpersonal trust and the mediating effect of social interactions. *Political Studies,* 56, 57-75.

Strauss, K. (2018). The 10 Companies with The Best CSR Reputations in 2017. Forbes.

Su, A.J. (2014). *The Questions Good Coaches Ask.* Retrieved from https://hbr.org/2014/12/the-questions-good-coaches-ask

Sustainability. Google. Retrieved from https://sustainability.google/

Tesla forecasts. Retrieved from https://www.teslaforecast.com/about-tesla/

Tesla (donation). Retrieved from https://www.mercurynews.com/2021/01/17/elon-musk-donates-5-million-to-mountain-view-based-education-group-khan-academy/

Thomas, D. (2009, September 30). *Explaining the Toyota Floormat Recall.* Retrieved from cars.com: https://www.cars.com/articles/2009/09/explaining-the-toyota-floormat-recall/

Thompson, J. (2017). *Lead true, live your values, build your people, inspire your community.* Forbes Books.

Thumma, S. A., & Beene, S. (2015). The judge as servant-leader. *Journal of Ethical Leadership, 54*(1), 9-13.

Trevino, L. K., Hartman, L. P., and Brown, M. (2000). Moral person and moral manager. California Management Review, 42(4), 128-142.

Vision and Values of Applebee's (2021). Retrieved from: The Applebee's® Restaurant Way–Our Vision & Values

Wallace, J. R. (2007). Servant leadership: A worldview perspective. International Journal of Leadership.

Walmart Core Values (2021) Retrieved from Walmart Core Values | Walmart Careers

Warfield, Kyle. (2020). Storm water management for congregations. Lutherans Restoring Creation. https://lutheransrestoringcreation.org/storm-water-management-for-congregations/

White, L. (1967). The historical roots of our ecological crisis. *Science,* 155(3767). 1203-1207.

Whyte, D. (2002). *The heart aroused: poetry and the preservation of the soul in corporate America.* Crown Publishing.

Wirzba, N. (2011). A priestly approach to environmental theology: learning to receive and give again the gifts of creation. *Dialog: A Journal of Theology,* 50(4), 354-362.

Wong, K. (2020, Aug 3). Core Company Values: 12 Inspiring Examples. Achievers: https://www.achievers.com/blog/company-core-value-examples/

Woodrum, E. & Hoban, D. (1994). Theology and religiosity effects on environmentalism. *Review of Religious Research,* 35(3), 193-206.

Wright, N. (1994). Jerusalem in the New Testament. *Jerusalem Past and Present in the Purposes of God,* P.W.L. Walker, Ed. Grand Rapids: Baker. 53-77.

Yang, S. Y. (2008). *A process views of wisdom.* Journal of Adult Development.

Yulk, G. et al. (2013). An improved measure of ethical leadership. Journal of Leadership and Organizational Studies, 20 (1), 38-48.

Appendix A - Leadership Inventory Assessment and Scores

Instructions: Read each item carefully and decide whether the item describes you as a person. Indicate your response to each item by circling one of the five numbers to the right of each item.

Key:	1 = Not true	2 = Seldom true	3 = Occasionally true	4 = Somewhat true	5 = Very true

1. I enjoy getting into the details of how things work.1 2 3 4 5
2. As a rule, adapting ideas to people's needs is easy for me.1 2 3 4 5
3. I enjoy working with abstract ideas.1 2 3 4 5
4. Technical things fascinate me.1 2 3 4 5
5. Understand others is the most important part of my work.1 2 3 4 5
6. Seeing the big picture comes easy for me.1 2 3 4 5
7. One of my skills is being good at making things work.1 2 3 4 5
8. My concern is to have a supportive communication climate.1 2 3 4 5
9. I am intrigued by complex organizational problems.1 2 3 4 5
10. Following directions and filling out forms comes easily for me.1 2 3 4 5
11. Understanding social fabric of the organization is important to me.1 2 3 4 5
12. I enjoy working out strategies for my organization's growth.1 2 3 4 5
13. I am good at completing the things I've been assigned to do.1 2 3 4 5
14. Getting all parties to work together is a challenge I enjoy.1 2 3 4 5
15. Creating a mission statement is rewarding work.1 2 3 4 5
16. I understand how to do the basic things required of me.1 2 3 4 5
17. I am concerned with how my decisions affect the lives of others.1 2 3 4 5
18. Thinking about organizational values & philosophy appeals to me.1 2 3 4 5

Scoring

The skills inventory is designed to measure three broad types of leadership skills: Technical, Human, and Conceptual. Score the questionnaire by doing the following. First, sum the responses on items 1, 4, 7, 10, 13, and 16. This is your technical skill score. Second, sum the responses on items 2, 5, 8, 11, 14, and 17. This is your human skill score. Third, sum the responses on items 3, 6 ,9, 12, 15, and 18. This is your conceptual skill score.

Technical skill (1, 4, 7, 10, 13, 16) ⎯⎯⎯⎯⎯
Human skill (2, 5, 8, 11, 14, 17) ⎯⎯⎯⎯⎯⎯
Conceptual skill (3, 6, 9, 12, 15, 18) ⎯⎯⎯⎯
Total Scores: ⎯⎯⎯⎯⎯⎯⎯⎯⎯⎯⎯⎯⎯

Scoring Interpretation

The scores you received on the skills inventory provide information about your leadership skills in three areas. By comparing the differences between your scores, you can determine where you have leadership strengths and where you have leadership weaknesses. Your scores also point toward the level of management for which you might be most suited.

Appendix B - Personal Assessment of Leaders (PAL)

Personal Assessment of Leadership (PAL) gives an overall profile of your level of skill competence. Please respond to the following statements (write the number that correspond to your rating scale to each statement) using the scale below:

Rating Scale:

1. Strongly disagree
2. Disagree
3. Slightly disagree
4. Slightly agree
5. Agree
6. Strongly agree

Self-Knowledge:

_____ 1. I seek information about my strengths and weaknesses from others as a basis for self-improvement.

_____ 2. In order to improve, I am willing to be self-disclosing to others, that is, to share my beliefs and feelings.

_____ 3. I am very much aware of my preferred style in gathering information and making decisions.

_____ 4. I have a good sense of how I cope with situations that are ambiguous and uncertain.

_____ 5. I have a well-developed set of personal standards and principles that guide my behavior.

Stressful or Time-Pressured situations:

_____ 6. I use effective time-management methods such as keeping track of my time, making to-to lists and prioritizing tasks.

_____ 7. I frequently affirm my priorities so that less important things don't drive out more important things.

_____ 8. I maintain a program of regular exercise for fitness.

_____ 9. I maintain an open and trusting relationship with someone with whom I can share my frustrations.

_____ 10. I know and practice several temporary relaxation techniques such as deep breathing and muscle relaxation.

_____ 11. I maintain balance in my life by pursuing a variety of interests outside of work.

Approach to a typical, routine problem.

_____ 12. I state clearly and explicitly what the problem is. I avoid trying to solve it until I have defined it.

_____ 13. I always generate more than one alternative solution to the problem, instead of identifying only one obvious solution.

_____ 14. I keep steps in the problem-solving process distinct; that is, I define the problem before proposing alternative solutions, and I generate alternatives before selecting a single solution.

When Faced with Complex Situation with No Easy Solution.

_____ 15. I try out several definitions of the problems. I don't limit myself to just one way to define it.

_____ 16. I try to unfreeze my thinking by asking lots of questions about the nature of the problem before considering ways to solve it.

_____ 17. I try to think about the problem from both the left (logical) side of my brain and the right (intuitive) side of my brain.

_____ 18. I do not evaluate the merits of an alternative solution to the problem before I have generated a list of alternatives. That is, I avoid deciding on a solution until I have developed many possible solutions.

_____ 19. I have some specific techniques that I use to help develop creative and innovative solutions to problems.

When trying to foster more creativity and innovation among those with whom I work.

_____ 20. I make sure there are divergent points of view represented or expressed in every complex problem-solving situation.

_____ 21. I try to acquire information from individuals outside the problem-solving group who will be affected by the decision, mainly to determine their preferences and expectations.

_____ 22. I try to provide recognition not only to those who come up with creative ideas (the idea champions) but also to those who support others' ideas (supporters) and who provide resources to implement them (orchestrators).

_____ 23. I encourage informed rule-breaking in pursuit of creative solutions.

_____ 24. I am able to help others recognize and define their own problems when I counsel them.

_____ 25. I am clear about when I should coach someone and when I should provide counseling instead.

_____ 26. When I give feedback to others, I avoid referring to personal characteristics and focus on problems or solutions instead.

_____ 27. When I try to correct someone's behavior, our relationship is about always strengthened.

_____ 28. I am descriptive in giving negative feedback to others. That is, I objectively describe events, their consequences, and my feelings about them.

_____ 29. I take responsibility for my statement and point of view by using, for example, "I have decided" instead of "They have decided."

_____ 30. I strive to identify some area of agreement in a discussion with someone who has a different point of view.

_____ 31. I don't talk down to those who have less power or less information than I.

_____ 32. When discussion someone's problem, I usually respond with a reply that indicates understanding rather than advice.

In a situation where it is important to obtain more power.

_____ 33. I always put forth more effort and take more initiative than expected in my work.

_____ 34. I am continually upgrading my skills and knowledge.

_____ 35. I strongly support organizational ceremonial events and activities.

_____ 36. I form a broad network of relationships with people throughout the organization at all levels.

_____ 37. In my work I consistently strive to generate new ideas, initiate new activities, and minimize routine tasks.

_____ 38. I consistently send personal notes to others when they accomplished something significant or when I pass along important information to them.

_____ 39. I refuse to bargain with individuals who use high-pressure negotiation tactics.

_____ 40. I always avoid using threats or demands to impose my will on others.

When another person needs to be motivated.

_____ 41. I always determine if the person has the necessary resources and support to succeed in a task.

_____ 42. I use a variety of rewards to reinforce exceptional performances.

_____ 43. I design task assignments to make them interesting and challenging.

_____ 44. I make sure the person gets timely feedback from those affected by task performance.

_____ 45. I always help the person establish performance goals that are challenging, specific, and time bound.

_____ 46. Only as a last resort do I attempt to reassign or release a poorly performance individual.

_____ 47. I consistently discipline when effort is below expectations and capabilities.

_____ 48. I make sure that people feel fairly and equitable treated.

_____ 49. I provide immediate compliments and other forms of recognition for meaningful accomplishments.

_____ 50. I avoid making personal accusations and attributing self-serving motives to the other person.

_____ 51. I encourage two-way interaction by inviting the respondent to express his or her perspective and to ask questions.

_____ 52. I make a specific request, detailing a more acceptable option.

When someone complains about something I've done.

_____ 53. I show genuine concern and interest, even when I disagree.

_____ 54. I seek additional information by asking questions that provide specific and descriptive information.

_____ 55. I ask the other person to suggest more acceptable behaviors.

When two people are in conflict and I am the mediator.

_____ 56. I do not take sides but remain neutral

_____ 57. I help the parties generate multiple alternatives.

_____ 58. I help the parties find areas on which they agree.

In situations where I have an opportunity to engage people in accomplishing work.

_____ 59. I help people feel competent in their work by recognizing and celebrating their small successes.

_____ 60. I provide regular feedback and need support.

_____ 61. I try to provide all the information that people need to accomplish their tasks.

_____ 62. I highlight the important impact that a person's work will have.

When engaging others in work.

_____ 63. I specify clearly the results I desire.

_____ 64. I specify clearly the level of initiative I want others to take (for example, wait for directions, do part of the task and then report, do the whole task and then report, and so forth).

_____ 65. I allow participation by those accepting assignments regarding when and how work will be done.

_____ 66. I avoid upward delegation by asking people to recommend solutions, rather than merely asking for advice or answers, when a problem is encountered.

_____ 67. I follow up and maintain accountability for delegated tasks on a regular basis.

When I am in the role of leader in a team.

_____ 68. I know how to establish credibility and influence among team members.

_____ 69. I am clear and consistent about what I want to achieve.

_____ 70. I build a common base of agreement in the team before moving forward with task accomplishment.

_____ 71. I articulate a clear, motivation vision of what the team can achieve along with specific shot-term goals.

When I am in the role of team member.

_____ 72. I know a variety of ways to facilitate task accomplishment in the team.

_____ 73. I know a variety of ways to help build strong relationships and cohesion among team members.

When I desire to make my team perform well, regardless of whether I am a leader or member.

_____ 74. I am knowledgeable about the different stages of team development experienced by most teams.

_____ 75. I help the team avoid groupthink by making sure that sufficient diversity of opinions is expressed in the team.

_____ 76. I can diagnose and capitalized on my team's core competencies, or unique strengths.

_____ 77. I encourage the team to achieve dramatic breakthrough innovations as well as small continues improvements.

When I am in a position to lead change.

_____ 78. I create possible energy in others when I interact with them.

_____ 79. I emphasize a higher purpose or meaning associated with the change I am leading.

_____ 80. I express gratitude frequently and conspicuously, even for small acts.

_____ 81. I emphasize building on strength, not just overcoming weaknesses.

_____ 82. I use a lot of more positive comments than negative comments.

_____ 83. When I communicate a vision, I capture people's hearts as well as their heads.

_____ 84. I know how to get people to commit to my vision of positive change.

Scoring Key

Skill Area	Items	Assessment Score (High/Low). High score on a skill means more competent. The opposite is true for low scores, which needs improvement.
Developing Self-awareness –Self-disclosure and openness –Awareness of self	**1-5** 1-2 3-5	
Managing Stress –Eliminating stressors –Developing resiliency –Short-term coping	**6-11** 6-7 8-9 10-11	

Solving Problems Creatively –Rational problem solving –Creative problem solving –Fostering innovation and creativity	**12-23** 12-14 15-19 20-23	
Communicating Supportively –Coaching and counseling –Effective negative feedback –Communicating supportively	**24-32** 24-25 26-28 29-32	
Gaining Power and Influence –Gaining power –Exercising influence	**33-40** 33-37 38-40	
Motivating Others	**41-49**	
Managing Conflict –Initiating –Responding –Mediating	**50-58** 50-52 53-55 56-58	
Empowering and Engaging –Empowering –Delegating	**59-67** 59-62 63-67	
Building Effective Teams and Teamwork –Leading teams –Team membership –Teamwork	**68-77** 68-71 72-73 74-77	
Leading Positive Change –Foster positive deviance –Lead positive change –Mobilize others	**78-84** 78-80 81-82 83-84	

Self-Assessment:

- Reflect on the assessment you just conducted.
- What category of score did you find interesting?
- What areas did you find challenging and needs improvement?
- How did you do on self-disclosure and openness? Questions 1-2
- How did you do on awareness of self? Questions 3-5
- Any surprises? Explain.
- Explain how you will build on your strength in the skill area on "Developing self-awareness"?

About This Book.

Servant Leaders are the greatest among us. Their humility and instinctively serviceable nature make them resourceful, go-to individuals, friends, advisors, mentors, and the memory of homes, communities, organizations, and countries. Yet, the path of servanthood to leadership is peculiar. Why serve first and lead second? Because serving is good work, hard work, noble work, and our work. Evidently, there is the difficulty of understanding research language and using them in leadership practices. This book fills that gap. Servant leadership is NOT an attitude. Neither is it only rooted in faith. It is a context-specific researched theory rooted in positivism. Servant leaders touch the souls of individuals and remain on their lips in every conversation. Do you want to be that kind of leader? Then, this book is for you. The future of next generational leadership could hinge on this book. Direct connection of servant leadership to career is the abundant need of such leaders in academia, nonprofit, police, military, politics, faith-based institutions, and the corporate world.

Topics in these fifteen chapters, well-researched book includes: Why Do We Need Servant Leaders? Can A Servant Lead? Understanding Theory in Servant Leadership Studies, Statistics in Theory–Don't Be Intimidated, Snapshot of Prevailing Leadership Theories Besides Servant Leadership, Servant Leadership–The Foundation, Servant Leadership–Other Perspectives, Servant Leadership and Building Community, Servant Leadership and Values; Interviews: 10 Questions for 11 Leaders of 11 Different Organizations, Servant Leadership and the Religious

Environment, Servant Leadership and Wisdom, Servant Leadership and Executive Coaching, Servant Leadership in the Boardroom, Servant Leadership and Ethics, Servant Leadership and Change, Steward Leadership and Servant Leadership, and Concluding Thoughts.

About the Author:

Dr. Enoch O. Antwi is a Leadership and Management Professor at Viterbo University, La Crosse, Wisconsin, USA. He designs and teaches servant leadership courses, including SVLD-330: Meaningful, Ethical and Practical Servant Leadership; SVLD 430: Mission, Vision and Virtues in Organizations, and SVLD 690: Colloquium, the final research paper in the only Master of Arts in Servant Leadership (MASL) program in the United States. Enoch is also the academic advisor of the MASL program. He is a leadership and management consultant, author of four books and a civic educationist. Dr. Antwi has a 22-year progressive academic and career experience spanning from media practitioner, international community development consulting, research fellow, manager in the corporate world, business ownership, business management program chair in a Career College and organizational leadership program chair at a Technical College, to a present traditional University professor. He enjoys travelling and loves watching football. Enoch is also the author of these books: Leadership is Concept Heavy: A Case Against Fragmented Theories in Evolutionary and Contemporary Leadership; Counting the Count in Business Consulting: Ideation of Top 40 Business Consultants; Political Party Followership and Political Leadership in Africa, and Hands-on Teaching and Evidence-based Learning in Africa.

CPSIA information can be obtained
at www.ICGtesting.com
Printed in the USA
LVHW022049120122
708426LV00011B/869